SAFE SEX: THE ANSWER TO YOUR QUESTIONS ABOUT HAPPY, HEALTHY EROTIC ENCOUNTERS FOR LIFE

—Doesn't safe sex really mean complete abstinence?

—How can I make intercourse a fulfilling and *safe* experience?

—Can I expand my erotic options while still protecting myself from sexually transmitted disease?

—How can I introduce a new sexual partner to safe sexual practice?

At a time when the question of sexual expression has become a matter of life and death for gay men, bisexuals, and the women who love them, sexual health consultant and writer John Preston and "Mr. Safesex," Glenn Swann, deliver the *good* news: that sex without fear need not be sex without excitement, stimulation, and passion. In this timely and provocative guide, they tell you why—and show you how!

JOHN PRESTON was trained as a sexual health consultant at the University of Minnesota Medical School program in Human Sexuality, and has been a managing editor at SIECUS. He has written numerous books on erotic fantasy, and writes regularly for *The Advocate* and other gay publications.

GLENN SWANN, an ex-Marine, has become internationally known as "Mr. Safesex," a pioneer for safe sexual practices.

JOHN PRESTON AND GLENN SWANN

SAFE SEX
THE ULTIMATE EROTIC GUIDE

With photographs by Fred Bissones

A PLUME BOOK

NEW AMERICAN LIBRARY

NEW YORK AND SCARBOROUGH, ONTARIO

NAL BOOKS ARE AVAILABLE AT QUANTITY DISCOUNTS WHEN USED
TO PROMOTE PRODUCTS OR SERVICES. FOR INFORMATION PLEASE
WRITE TO PREMIUM MARKETING DIVISION, NEW AMERICAN
LIBRARY, 1633 BROADWAY, NEW YORK, NEW YORK 10019.

 PLUME TRADEMARK REG. U.S. PAT. OFF. AND FOREIGN COUNTRIES
REGISTERED TRADEMARK—MARCA REGISTRADA
HECHO EN CHICAGO, U.S.A.

SIGNET, SIGNET CLASSIC, MENTOR, ONYX, PLUME, MERIDIAN AND NAL BOOKS
are published *in the United States* by New American Library,
1633 Broadway, New York, New York 10019, *in Canada* by
The New American Library of Canada, Limited,
81 Mack Avenue, Scarborough, Ontario M1L 1M8

Library of Congress Cataloging-in-Publication Data

Preston, John.
  Safe sex.

  1. Sex instruction for homosexual men. 2. Safe sex
in AIDS prevention. 3. AIDS (Disease)—Prevention.
I. Swann, Glenn. II. Title.
HQ76.1.P74 1987   613.9'5   86–20502
ISBN 0–452–25896–0

Designed by Leonard Telesca

First Printing, January, 1987

1 2 3 4 5 6 7 8 9

PRINTED IN THE UNITED STATES OF AMERICA

CONTENTS

FOREWORD

Sex does not cause AIDS.

Some sexual practices help transmit AIDS.

Those are the two basic messages that we have to get to sexually active people during the current health crisis. They're simple; they're straightforward; they give us the building blocks to help protect against the spread of the disease and still continue to lead fulfilling lives.

But making that point hasn't been easy. There have been enormous roadblocks put up in the area of AIDS education. The essential problem is obvious: AIDS can be sexually transmitted.

For one thing, that means we have to discuss it in terms that can be easily understood. But unfortunately the media and the federal government have problems talking plainly about sex. "Some people are going to have to be offended," said *The Economist* magazine in a February 1986 editorial— but it took a long time for the press to get that message.

In fact, before even New York and Boston papers were ready to address the issues involved with AIDS, my own home state's largest daily newspaper, the Portland *Press–Herald,* editorialized in 1984 that AIDS had to be recognized as the nation's number-one health priority. Unhappily, the parent company of the newspaper wasn't about to be a part of the response. The statewide gay periodical, *Our Paper,* had been printed in a plant owned by the corporation. When the pressmen objected that safe-sex guidelines included in an AIDS article were "pornographic," management decided to let its employees dictate policy. Ignoring its own proclamation of a crisis, it refused to print the offending issue.

That attitude has been in force in the government as well. After the Centers for Disease Control (CDC) recognized that altering gay male sexual behavior was one of the most important steps in the battle against AIDS, it invited grant applications in 1986 from various groups for programs that could reach that population with safe-sex messages. This posed a problem: In order to encourage people to avoid certain sexual acts, alternatives had to be proposed. That meant the government would have to be in the position of promoting homosexual behavior. As one might expect, the right wing was not pleased.

The medical necessity was so obvious and so imperative, though, that the CDC kept on going with its idea for some time. Even in the face of criticism, it was ready, it seemed, to stick to the project. Then another, more difficult issue came to the fore: The educational materials that would be most effective were going to have to be explicit. The government not only would be validating some homosexual acts, but also it would be financing the production of "pornographic" materials to advocate them.

That was too much. Rather than focus on the validity of the content and the efficacy of the message, the CDC now decided that the materials the various groups produced had to go through local review panels. And these reviewing bodies were not comprised of the people to whom the materials were directed but were drawn from the "larger community."

The result was, in no uncertain terms, a farce. While the government now acknowledges that a large population is "at risk" to the fatal AIDS virus, it insists that the sensibilities of others be the most important concern in its education materials.

Still, even faced with these barriers, many of us have been actively involved in trying to spread the message of safe sex to those people who so vitally need to hear it. It has not been easy. We've discovered a number of other roadblocks to the task.

To begin with, scientists are confused—and confusing. And after listening to an official of the National Institutes of Health and a professor from Harvard University break out in an acrimonious public debate on prime-time television about just how the disease is spread sexually, I understood just why scientists face an increasing lack of credibility among gay men and others. It is difficult to get clear answers and to sift our way through the evidence that's presented to us by a group that doesn't always seem to speak English.

In the end, however, there are certain commonsense observations that most researchers will stand by. These make up the foundation for what we call safe sex. All of these observations come back to one enormous probability: that AIDS is transmitted by an exchange of semen and/or blood between people. Because of this, certain rules are irrefutable:

1. *Do not ingest semen.* You should not engage in oral intercourse (sucking; giving head) to the point of orgasm. The great probability is that seminal fluid allows

the AIDS virus to travel between two people. Swallow-
ing that fluid (cum), is too dangerous.

2. *Do not engage in anal intercourse without a condom.*
   The introduction of semen into the anus—especially in
   large amounts—is extremely dangerous. If you fuck, you
   must use a condom to stop the seminal fluid from entering the other person's body.

3. *Do not drink urine.* Water sports are too dangerous.
   Many of the "opportunistic infections"—those diseases
   that infect people with AIDS—can be transmitted too
   easily via piss.

4. *Do not use your partner's sex toys.* AIDS evidently can
   survive outside the body for a long time. A sexual appa-
   ratus that's been used on one person who's been in-
   fected can harbor the virus, which can then be spread to
   another. Cleaning reduces this probability, but it must
   be *very* thorough.

5. *Do not rim.* There's no question that oral/anal contact is
   a highly effective way for disease to spread. It's definitely a major means of transmitting hepatitis. It is
   absolutely the quickest way to exchange parasites. It
   very probably can spread AIDS.

Are you shocked to see these words published in a main-
stream book? Well, now you know why the government and
the media have had their problems. But it doesn't alter the
very essential fact that this is the kind of information that has
got to be talked about in an open and honest manner if we're
going to fight AIDS.

Some people wonder, when they listen to the lists of
health warnings, why gay men—and other sexually active
people—don't just stop having sex. That was indeed the
advice given by a number of medical people when the epidemic was first recognized. The assumptions behind the

question don't reflect the reality that sex is an important function in human life. It brings to us much more than a simple experience of orgasm.

That's especially true for gay men, most of whom have gone through long and extraordinarily painful periods of denying their sexuality. The sensationalistic reports of the "promiscuity" of gay male life doesn't have much to do with the day-to-day reality of how most homosexual men live. But it does reflect the period of "coming out" and, with it, the "breaking out" of the periods of suppression that a majority of gay men report as a transition.

The memories of those periods of self-denial convince many gay men that the power and right to engage in sexual behavior is too important to be abandoned.

"Well, then," many medical personnel responded, "just become monogamous." That often-repeated advice is the best piece of evidence I've seen that medical education doesn't have enough of a basis in human reality. It would have seemed obvious by now—with the census statistics concerning the soaring divorce rate and the increase in single-parent families in the U.S. today, that people cannot "will" themselves a partner for life.

The constant bombardment of impractical and unnecessarily pessimistic "advice" has led many people—*not just gay men*—to ignore and to dismiss all the counsel they've heard. Combined with a strong, even if irrational, desire to deny the dangers, too many people have given up on the idea of changing their behavior.

We can't change all of our psychological predispositions, any more than we can change all of the cultural forces that act upon us. But we *can* change our behavior. And doing so doesn't *have* to mean giving into unrealistic morality or forgoing physical, romantic, and emotional pleasure. That theory is the basis of safe sex.

The movement to spread that educational message has been largely confined to the gay world. It makes sense in some ways. Homosexually active men remain one of the two major populations at risk for acquiring the disease, along with intravenous drug users.

At one point, when arguments were being made concerning the CDC educational grants, it seemed that many people believed the gay community could provide that education by itself. Certainly gay organizations raised—and continue to raise—a great deal of money for other aspects of AIDS education and AIDS care. There exists a network of gay newspapers and magazines, most of which have begun to advocate safe sex in their pages.

But to keep education the responsibility of the gay community assumes that all homosexually active men are gay, belong to gay organizations, read gay periodicals, attend gay meetings and seminars. That's simply not true. In fact, the percentage of men who engage in homosexual acts who identify with the gay community is minuscule.

Remember: The Kinsey statistics speculate that at least 10% of the male population has adult homosexual experience. If all of those people were actively gay, there certainly would be a lot more gay legislation passed in this country.

It's also true that many gay organizations are political in a way that turns off even many gay men. While the public appearance of lobbying groups and other media advocates may present an image of a powerful gay lobby, those organizations and individuals often don't have a large constituency behind them.

This all combines to make the process of safe-sex education all the more difficult. While those of us involved in the movement could go from meeting to meeting, we knew that we were, after a certain point, speaking to the converted. We had to reach other homosexually active men who saw their genital activity as only a sexual component of their lives, not as a social or political identity.

How could we do it? Well, one of the most effective means that I found was to do precisely what the right-wing moralists were accusing us of doing: produce pornography.

Most of the original warnings given to sexually active people concentrated on a list of proscriptions, of dont's absolute and so rigid that they were dismissed by all but the most panic-stricken and defeatist people who read them. The inability to create a new, positive approach to sexuality meant that people just couldn't live with it at all.

The first step, then, was to create a positive image for safe-sex acts. Those of us who could write erotica and get it published suddenly found ourselves as interested in making it desirable as we were in communicating its disease-preventative need.

We accomplished something more. We were getting the safe-sex message into publications that were read by a whole different population than those who were reading politically based newspapers. The fact is, a lot more people out there read and learn from *Advocate Men* and *Mandate* than by studying *Gay Community News* or *The New York Native*.

As I became more and more involved in this project, I grew aware of larger and larger parts of the population that still weren't being reached.

For example, there are the men who frequent rest rooms for sex. Laud Humphreys won many professional awards—and an equal amount of professional controversy—when he published a book called *Tea Room Trade*. He documented that most of the men who engaged in sex in "tea rooms" —public rest rooms—weren't, by any definition, *gay*. They tended to be married, in fact, and used the homosexual outlet for nothing but orgasmic release.

The men who go to public rest rooms for sex are an

extreme. But they share a great deal with other men who, as the most sexually active, are thus the most crucial for us to reach. These men inhabited the back rooms of porn shops, the audiences of adult theaters, and the orgy rooms of bathhouses. They were people who were avoiding all personal content in their sexual life because they were frightened of being identified as homosexual.

About the time that I was involved in talking to a number of other people active in the safe-sex movement about this particular—and enormous—problem, I became aware of Glenn Swann.

I'd read about someone who called himself "Mr. Safe Sex" in *The Weekly News,* a gay newspaper published in Miami. He intrigued me. I wrote and offered to interview him. As we talked that first time I realized that this guy was out there doing the things that no one else had been able to accomplish.

He was performing his act in adult theaters and in bathhouses (both the traditional ones and in newly restructured ones, such as Jack Campbell's Club Body Centers). I not only did the telephone interview, I arranged to meet Glenn and to see how he accomplished this.

Glenn's delivery, I discovered, is blunt and to the point. He stands in front of an audience and, always speaking in the language they can understand, he speaks directly to them about the need to embrace safe sex. His message isn't just that it has to be done but also that it can be fun.

You can watch an assembly of men as they listen to Glenn and understand that they're very likely listening for the first time to a spokesman, and trusting him. For Glenn has both the image they respect, a personality they want, and an authenticity with which they can identify just as easily as they can spot a fake.

I was impressed enough to approach Glenn about the idea

of doing this book together. I felt that if we could use erotic fantasy to describe and highlight the process he had gone through to arrive at his place of endorsing safe sex so enthusiastically, then we could give to the people an important document about how to have sex during the health crisis. Between us I felt that we could present something that would appeal to a wide-ranging audience.

Certainly there are still politically and socially involved gay people who are looking for more reinforcement for their safe-sex practices. There are those others whom Glenn reaches in his stage presentations who would read a book like this one but never approach what they perceived as a "gay liberation" tract.

There's also the very obvious fact that gay men aren't the only ones interested in the ideas of safe sex anymore. As more and more evidence spreads about the probability of heterosexual transmission of AIDS, then more and more people of all sexualities want to understand what's involved in this alteration of sexual activity.

It was important, then, that we be able to distribute the work as thoroughly as possible. If it was limited to a few gay bookstores, the purpose wouldn't be fulfilled. We would be in danger of preaching to the converted once more.

To be honest, I wasn't very optimistic about the possibility of a large publishing house doing this book. But we were determined at least to try to have it published as widely as possible, and the response was, to say the least, gratifying. We have done our best to put together the best guide to the joys of safe sex that we can. With the encouragement of our publisher and editor we're assured that it will be put out there for those people who are interested and who need to understand what's involved in this new chapter in our sexual lives.

But, given all the discouragement I've described in facing

this process of safe-sex education, can I really expect there to be that kind of impact? Can books like this and the repeated message of the need to change something as fundamental as how we have sex with another really reach people?

Here's a possible answer: I recently came back home from a long and particularly discouraging trip. I dropped my bags in my apartment, walked up the street to the local gay bar, and took a drink from the owner, Mary. Having heard all the hard stories before, Mary was still as sympathetic as ever while I described the resistance I had faced in Los Angeles to the ideas behind safe sex. L.A. was a city where I would have expected more people to understand what was happening and what needed to be changed, but I could see little consciousness and a lot of denial.

A man standing beside me was listening to our conversation. I wasn't paying any special attention to him, though I noticed that he was being carefully appreciated by someone on the other end of the bar. When I was finished talking, and before Mary could deliver her own thoughts, my neighbor reached into his back pocket and pulled out a wrapped condom. He slapped it on the bar. "It's like those bankers and their American Express cards," he declared. "I don't leave home without it!" Then he turned to his admirer. "And if you don't like it, just stop looking at my ass."

That, friends, is AIDS awareness, and that's the attitude that's going to help us fight the spread of this disease.

John Preston
Portland, Maine

INTRODUCTION

The main thing I got out of the Marine Corps was that buddies helped their buddies.

Whatever else you want to say about the service, it does teach you that you're part of a team. What you and every other man in that team does is an important element in its success or failure. My years in the Corps had their ups and downs—I'm not going to turn it into a fantasy of pure delight—but my time in uniform did teach me that lesson.

When I came back to the States as a civilian, I made my way into the gay community. Just when it seemed that my network of friends was getting itself together, AIDS hit. I saw some buddies get sick, and I knew that I wanted to help. But I didn't know how.

I didn't have any training in medicine. I didn't know what I could possibly do to give a hand in the middle of the crisis. In this society it's easy to put yourself down. If you don't have a formal education with a line of initials after your name, people don't want to take you very seriously. You can join in marches; they have their purpose. You can write letters to Congress—and lots of us did that. But I was left with a sense of powerlessness. What could I possibly offer?

I had done a number of sexual films and posed for gay magazines; I was proud of my body and happy that it gave me a way to earn a few dollars. Yet it didn't seem that this was a real way to have any effect on a *health* crisis. Most people seem to think that anyone with muscles is just a dumb jock, and that impression's only intensified if you show them off in front of a camera.

There just didn't seem to be any way that I could help out the guys on my new team who were in trouble. Like so many other people, I just withdrew into a cocoon, feeling scared and feeble as the newspaper headlines kept getting larger and the numbers in the reports got bigger.

Maybe the worst part of all was the idea some people had that I was actually part of the problem! Since I was appearing in sexually oriented movies and photo spreads, some people thought I was encouraging gay men to go out and have dangerous sex.

That didn't feel right at all. It made no sense to me. If someone was sitting home and having a good time with his fantasies in a magazine or on a videocassette, then he was doing the safest thing there was—having fun by himself. But the accusations hurt.

I was also confused. Every time I turned on the television or went to a speech, the contradictions I heard in the reports about the causes of AIDS only made me more bewildered.

The most encouraging piece of the puzzle was the possibility that there was some kind of "safer sex" out there. I got some pamphlets and listened to some AIDS activists talking, I saw that this might be true; it could be something that could work.

Then, one day, I met up with Jack Campbell, the founder of the Club Baths chain. The baths were under attack from a lot of parties. They were seen as these dark dens of iniquity where people were having wild sex that was threatening their lives.

Jack had taken those clubs he owned personally and removed them from the Club Baths chain. He'd renamed them Club Body Centers. What difference did a name make? Jack explained that the areas of the clubs that encouraged anonymous sex had been removed, and bodybuilding centers equipped for real workouts were now in their place. These clubs had become centers of educational programs and other community activities. The company even had underwritten the cost of brochures promoting safe sex.

That's why he was talking to me.

It seemed that Jack was having a hard time convincing a lot of gay men that they had to change their sexual habits during the epidemic. Some things just wouldn't be possible anymore, and there were other things we all had to learn. He wanted me to take my public personality as an erotic star and use it as the theme of his educational campaigns. He wanted me to become Mr. Safe Sex.

I wasn't sure about this idea at all. From what he'd said, I knew that it would involve a lot of public appearances and even sexual performances. "I have a lot of thinking to do about this," I told him. I was going to have to give up my private life and spend a lot of time on the road. But, as he talked more and more, I realized that this just might be the answer I was looking for. It might be the way I could play my part in the whole arena. Maybe I wasn't a doctor or a nurse or a teacher or a scientist, but I had some talents and some experiences, and I could use them to help my buddies— just the way I'd been taught in the Marine Corps.

I have to admit that my problems with the idea of promoting myself as Mr. Safe Sex were very similar to the hassles that other gay men had about safe sex. Sometimes it seemed to me that all you were allowed to do was to stand in a corner and jerk off with your best friend and that was it.

Did our options really have to be that limited? Thinking about it, I realized that it wasn't just that safe sex was presented as such a negative thing—the definition of safe sex was almost always a list of all the things you *couldn't* do. There was something else involved: It was just no fun. Gay men had defined sex so narrowly that when the few things we said we wanted to do were taken away, there was almost nothing left.

I thought about that a lot, and I had to admit that my own sexuality—even when I was performing in erotic movies—was pretty much limited to what my cock did, and sometimes my ass. No matter that I worked on the rest of my body all the time in the gym; I didn't pay that much attention to it in erotic terms.

If a new outlook on sex was going to work at all, then sex had to be something that involved more than putting my penis in something or getting someone else's penis in my own body.

To tell the truth, that frightened me. I think such a big change might be something that scares a lot of men. Think about it: If you're just into regular fucking, then you really don't have to work all that hard to have an orgasm. It's easy enough to learn to play one note on a musical instrument; it's a lot harder to put those notes into a melody.

But that was the whole thing, I realized: If you knew how to construct a song, then you also could invent different tunes to play for different occasions. Maybe a hot disco number was what you'd like to hear most often, but if disco was suddenly dangerous, it didn't mean that letting loose with some fine jazz couldn't give you a lot of pleasure.

Maybe, I thought, people would start to like safe sex if they started thinking of it that way. Perhaps I could teach them to make such good music with some alternatives that we could get on with our life, still having decent sex and also going about the business that had to be done in the rest of the health crisis.

I was beginning to like the idea of being Mr. Safe Sex a lot more. But I knew that if I was going to do this, I wanted to do it right. Before I'd take up Jack's offer to go on the road, I decided I'd have to learn a lot more about my own body and my own sexuality. For someone in his mid-twenties who'd started a career as a porn star, it seemed strange—but it was true.

I had to face the fact that most of the sex I had was a race to an orgasm. Maybe I could hold back the orgasm for a bit to help out my partner; I certainly had to do that on camera sometimes to satisfy the director. But I had to admit that the major theme in my sex life was getting it off. I *loved* doing it that way; I won't lie and say it wasn't true. But that disco number just wasn't going to work anymore; I had to learn how to play some very cool jazz.

How was I going to move beyond the obvious drive to orgasm and learn how to make my own sex life more enjoyable? What limitations had I placed on my own erotic responses? If I could answer these questions and learn to teach other people what I'd discovered, then I'd be making the contribution I'd been looking to do all along, helping us all out.

What follows is a story based on my own series of erotic and "educational" adventures. It begins with the learning I had to do to become Mr. Safe Sex and then moves on to the life I've been leading once it all fell into place.

My first adventure began because I knew I had to start by learning more about my body and how it felt to have other people touch it. There had been a lot of men, and some women, in my life who I had thought were *experts* at *that*. But, as I said, all of the attention we'd paid had been to only small parts of our anatomy, and all that pleasure had been fixated on one goal: fast and furious orgasm.

I asked people who I knew were into safe sex how they'd gotten going on it? What was their starting point? The answer made them all dreamy-eyed: they told me that massage was one of the keys.

Did that mean going to a local massage parlor and getting a man or woman to give them a hand job? I wondered. That seemed a pretty lousy way to start off, and it was just the opposite of what I was after. All that did was use a hand to do what some other part of the body had been accomplishing.

"No, no," my friends insisted. "You have to get a *real* massage."

They told me that Karl, someone I knew from my local gymnasium, was an expert at it. Well, it was worth a try, I thought. But I felt certain . . . hesitations about putting my body into Karl's grip. Still, I decided that if that was the way to go, I'd do it. I was committed to the whole program. I called him up and made an appointment. It was time to start.

Glenn Swann
Miami, Florida

SAFE SEX

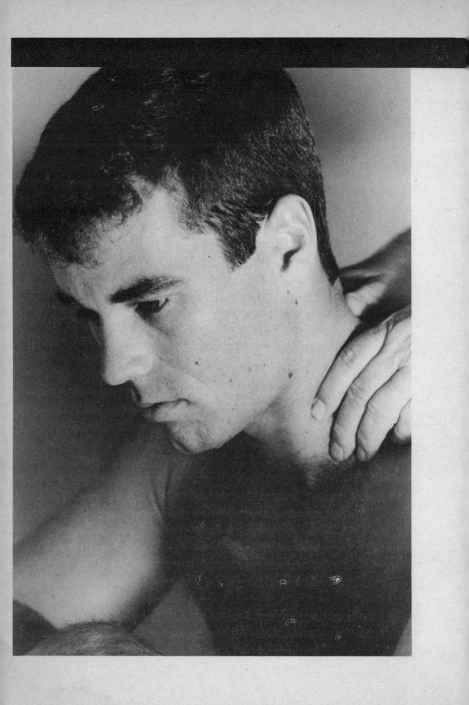

CHAPTER ONE

GETTING IN TOUCH

"Is this going to hurt?" I asked Karl as I got up on the massage table.

The big weight lifter was obviously surprised by my question. "Why would you think it would hurt?"

"Well, the only times I've ever gotten a rubdown were from trainers in the locker room or else medics in the Marine Corps. They weren't exactly interested in creating an erotic experience."

The big Swede laughed. "Not to worry, Glenn. This isn't the same thing, not at all. Now, you say you want to learn about massage, right? I'll explain as much as I can as I go along."

Just how serious was Karl? I wondered when he turned down the lights. I had been honest with him about what I wanted, and I wasn't sure why he was setting the scene for a seduction.

"Remember, there are many types of body relaxation," he said. "You can learn any of them. A very few—rolfing is one example—are too complicated and dangerous for untrained people to try, but basic massage is simple.

"Most massage can be done on the floor or on a bed. But anyone who wants to really use it should buy a table. You need the height to be able to use your whole body while you're performing on someone else's.

"Begin with a good oil. You can buy some commercial massage oils at many different stores. Me, I like almond oil. It has the benefit of not drying up on your skin too easily. Also, it doesn't absorb quickly.

"There are others. Lanolin is an ingredient in many mixtures. It comes from wool. Avocado actually has vitamins that the body can take in through the skin. You'll also find coconut, apricot, and wheat-germ oils for sale.

"Of course, many of them have another advantage: They're edible. If you're with someone else"—he laughed again—"that could make a difference. You'll have to make your own taste tests, though. It's a matter of personal preference.

"Any oil will do the job. Some of the glycerin-based lotions you can buy in drugstores are fine, but they work into the skin and you have to constantly pour on more. The best ones don't absorb too quickly. That's good, because it means that your hands glide over the surface and don't cause friction.

"Now, lie down on the table, on your back, and we'll start."

I sprawled out and waited. I was still a little bit tense, not really knowing what to expect from this. But I had been told that Karl was the best in the business, so I was determined to let him do his work.

"Now, before we start with the oil, it's always good to work out some of the tension in the head." He put his fingertips on my temples and began to press on them lightly, with slow, circular motions.

The minute he began his work, I understood just why he was so confident of the ability of the massage to do its job. The worry just seemed to *melt* out of me. Forgetting that I was interested in being taught about the erotic possibilities of all this, I just fell into the pleasure I was receiving. He moved his fingers down under my chin, then back up my head to work on my skull. He was pressing hard, but this certainly wasn't at all painful.

"There, now you're getting in the mood." He was right, but I wished he hadn't stopped. I was more interested in just continuing exactly what he'd been doing than in moving on to something else.

"One of the secrets," he said, starting up again, "is to continue to work on one part of the body. Amateurs most often want to move too quickly. They should always stay in one place for longer than they imagine."

Well, that certainly fit into how I was feeling. I wanted this to go on for a long, long time.

I had no idea how much time Karl had worked on my head. When his hands left me, I was even more aware of how enjoyable his touch had been. It had seemed to have calmed me so much that I'd gone into what felt like a slight hypnotic trance.

I looked over at him. I was already so unwound that my feelings seemed to be moving in slow motion. I saw him holding his hands cupped together. "The most common mistake in using oils," Karl explained, "is to put the liquid right on the body. It's almost always too cold. If you put it onto the skin straight from the container, it gives the other person a little jolt, and that's just what you're trying to avoid.

"Sometimes you can heat the oil in its bottle by placing it in hot water. Or, it's easier simply to hold it in your hands and let your own body heat warm it up."

I was aware of something else that was going on: Karl was speaking in a low, calm voice. The sounds he was making obviously were designed to mesh with the physical effect he wanted his actions to have. Now the low lights made more sense to me. It was my own narrow mind that assumed this all had to be headed in one direction. These elements were all really just parts of creating a relaxing atmosphere. Sure, they could lead to sex, but they didn't have to be going in that direction.

And, just as important, I realized my own part in this: Even if Karl had made some move that I didn't want to respond to, I could simply say no. It wasn't what I'd agreed to do; I'd only asked for a massage. Another important lesson: You can turn down a request for more than you want. I bet that a lot of gay men feel badly about that. You might agree to do something sensible and then discover that your partner won't be satisfied without trying for something else.

If you trust a guy—and I knew I should be able to trust Karl—then you don't have to be waiting every single minute to be forced to compromise what you want to do. I had a right to sink into Karl's hands and let go of the worry. If I had to, I could reach down inside and stop things. But you have to be willing to risk other people's good intentions at some point.

Karl moved back over to me, and I felt slippery lotion being applied to my chest. He smeared it over the whole upper half of my torso in quick, smooth motions. "Remember, I told you that some oils can be too quickly drunk up by the skin," Karl said. "This oil—designed for massage—will stay on the surface for a long time. That's why I can leave it on so much of the body while I work on specific parts.

"This is another reason for the room you massage in to be warmer than you normally might have it. When the other person is nude—especially when there are liquids on him—a cool room will leave him uncomfortable."

I tried to remember these facts as he began to knead at my shoulders. His deep motions were digging into my muscles, and I resisted at first. "Relax," he whispered. "You're fighting me." And I was. I was still expecting him to go at me the way those trainers had when I had leg cramps. But I was here to learn this time, and I willed my body not to tighten up.

As soon as I did, everything became a lot more mellow. Without the hardened and resisting defenses I'd been holding on to, Karl's fingers weren't feeling like they were digging into me at all anymore. Instead, they were working with me, working away at the tensions and helping the anxieties flee.

After he was satisfied that my shoulders were in good shape, Karl moved down my right arm. I felt my biceps go through the same process of trying to withstand the assault they were anticipating. But as soon as I stopped them, there was no competition at all, just the soothing touch of Karl's well-trained fingers.

By the time he'd reached my forearms, I was into the whole thing so much that I could let my arm go lax without combatting him at all.

As he finished each one of the parts Karl would take his palm and press down at the top, near the shoulder. He'd use a sweeping motion to move it along the entire length of my arm.

"Keep your eyes closed," he said when he saw me trying to study his actions. "You'll just divert your attention if you let too many of your senses get involved. Let this just be touch."

His warning came just in time. It turned out that he was about to start one of the best elements of the massage now. He'd moved down to my hand. Taking it in both of his own larger hands, he began to work his thumbs against my palm. Then he took my fingers and gave each one special attention.

It was wonderful. I'd begun wanting to teach myself that my cock and my ass weren't the whole of my sexuality. By the time Karl was done with my fingers, I was convinced that each of them was a sexual organ in its own right.

I don't mean that it just felt *good,* or that my hands felt sensual in some abstract way—what Karl was doing was totally sexual. I had the proof in the way my cock was bouncing up and down on my belly now. The man had made me so aware of my body's sensations that I had gotten hard.

I nearly sighed out loud when he carefully placed my hand back on the edge of the massage table. I was vaguely aware of his movements as he went over to the other side and started to work on the other arm. My cock wasn't going to go down while it waited for that special attention to my left fingers.

"Stay relaxed," Karl said as he began to work on my front. He worked easily on my chest, rubbing in toward my heart with the flat of his hands. He was lighter when he got to my belly. "Here, you must be careful," his slightly accented voice said. "There aren't that many strong muscles and no bones to protect the organs."

He continued to work. Sometimes, in the larger muscles such as those in my thighs, he would dig harder; when he was close to my major bones, he would also work the muscles more intensely, as though he wanted to free them from my skeleton.

"Here is one of the secrets you might learn," Karl said as he started to work on my knees. "This is one of the great erogenous zones that people never seem to pay enough attention to."

As his hands began to go to work on the back of my knee, little electric shocks seemed to go off all around them. It turned out that the small area is a hotbed of nerve endings. Karl was right, it was *very* sensual.

When he started to work on my calves, I was reminded of most of the locker-room experiences I had remembered. By this time, though, I was so relaxed that I only paid attention to the way his fingers seemed to soften the hardness of my tendons.

Then he got to my feet!

If I had thought that the massage had worked wonders on my hands, now it performed miracles. The touch of Karl's thumbs as they worked on my soles was amazing. At first I was very self-conscious; I was worried that he'd tickle me, or that that skin on the bottom of my feet would be so rough and unattractive that he'd say something.

In fact, there was a sandpapery feel when his hands and my feet were in contact at first. But Karl had seen dozens— hundreds—of feet, and he wasn't concerned about the knobs on my toe joints or how coarse the skin was. That was just another piece of the baggage I'd brought into this, and I soon convinced myself to let go of it.

"In massage it's important that the person never be forced back to full consciousness while it's happening," he said in a soft voice, finishing up. "But you must turn over now. Take your time. Don't move with any quick motions. Roll your body gently. It might help if you keep your eyes closed while you do it." I followed his instructions and took a couple of minutes to complete the maneuver.

Now he began the whole thing over again, starting with my shoulders and sweeping down over my back. He was especially careful above my waist where I knew the kidneys were close to the surface. With each part of my body he would repeat his pattern: He'd pay particular attention to a small area, massaging it in depth and for a long time—though it was never long enough for me—and then he would sweep his hands over a much larger area.

When he was working on one of my legs or my arms, he would seem to be pushing everything toward the extremities, as though he could just physically force the tension and anxiety out of my body that way. When he was working on the main part of my torso—my chest, back, and stomach—he seemed to want to move all of my blood back to my heart. That was his target area, at least.

I'd been aware that he had avoided my hard cock and my balls when he'd done my front side. He wasn't in business to give a hand-job, after all. By now, though, the sensations of my body were so dispersed over the whole of my torso that the pressure of having my whole weight on my erection just added to my pleasure.

When he got to my buttocks, Karl went to town. He kneaded them hard, making me aware of the flexibility of my ass and—unlike his avoidance of my genitals—he had no hesitations about using the cleft between the two parts of my behind to get a good grip. The fingers that pressed against the bottom of the ravine in the middle of my ass were a strangely benign intrusion into that usually hidden part of my body.

He worked his wonders on the back of my thighs. Then, again he was manipulating the back of my knees, and that special sensation swept over me. Back to my calves and finally to my feet again.

Following his own good advice, Karl had gone slowly the whole while. By the time he was finished, I was so relaxed, I felt half asleep. I know I had a stupid grin on my face. I just wanted to go right into full-fledged slumber. Well, maybe I wouldn't have minded jerking off a bit first. But Karl wasn't finished with his lessons.

"Human hands are the best for this purpose. But there are machines that can be used to very good effect in massage. I brought some here to show you."

I stayed where I was on my stomach and heard the click of an appliance being turned on. There was a slight, subdued whir. "This is perhaps the most common." He brought it to the head of the table to show me. "It's called a 'wand massager.' Almost all of the electronic companies sell them in one model or another. It has a long handle, as you can see, and the head vibrates rapidly. Let me show you. . . ."

Karl applied the rapidly trembling round top to the edge of one of my shoulders. I'm not sure what I really expected. What I got was a feeling that came close to matching the soft, high-action sound. As he moved the head across my back the machine left a trail of highly sensitized and highly eroticized skin behind it.

I didn't like feeling it move away and then turn off any more than I had liked the end of my physical massage. "Now, this is a different kind of machine. It has two heads and it's designed for larger muscle masses."

I don't think I appreciated the implication of just what were my largest "muscle masses" when, after the second machine was turned on, I felt it descend on my ass. But there was no doubt that the device was able to do its job. It seemed to work more deeply than the wand had, affecting my actual muscles more than the other machines which mainly had been pleasurable on the surface of my skin.

"People think that vibrators are like dirty toys, things that can only be used for insertion into the body's orifices—the vagina, the anus. There are plenty made for that purpose. You can get them yourself, and you'll have no trouble learning how to use them. But the best vibrators, like these, are for the entire body—just the way the best sex is for the entire body.

"You don't have to use the machines, either. Here is another massage tool that works well." Karl was holding something that looked like a toy car, but one with oversized wheels. He put it on my back and began to roll it up and down my body, with the wheels on either side of my spine.

He lifted them up and brought them back up, almost to

my neck. "Don't just move back and forth on the torso,"
Karl said. "Move away from the head, drawing the tension
away from it and out of the body—even if only symbolically.

"You can get something like this, which you can use on
yourself," he said. "It has a number of small globes that are
held together by string. There are handles that allow you to
move it over your back as well as your leg muscles and the
muscles at the front of your body. Others are designed
specifically for the feet. Most cities have health stores that
carry a large selection, and the staff can show you the
possibilities.

"We're finished," he said when he was done with the
massage machine.

I moved to swing my feet off the table. I felt rubbery, as
though the muscles in my body weren't working to their full
ability. Then I realized that that was exactly it. They were
reacting just the way they were supposed to after such a
thorough relaxation.

Well, most of them were. . . .

"That you will have to take care of in the privacy of your
own home." Karl smirked. "You will have to take the things
I've taught you here today and experiment with them on
your own body. Then, eventually you will be able to take
them to another person and use them for this new sexuality
of yours."

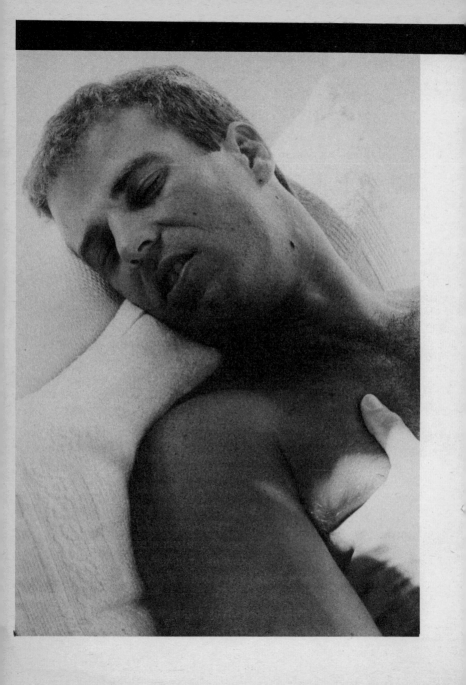

CHAPTER TWO

A DIFFERENT DRUMMER

After I was finished at Karl's studio I just went home and enjoyed the calm and the lingering pleasures of the massage. I sipped a single glass of wine and listened to some good music on the stereo.

I did do one thing that was different: When I got home, I stripped down to nothing. It seemed as though my skin felt so great that I didn't want to have clothing next to it; I especially didn't want to have the elastic bands of underwear and shorts binding me. I didn't think a lot about it at first. But later on, when I realized that I wasn't used to getting this kind of enjoyment out of my entire body, I had to smile.

I made myself take this all slow and easy. . . .

I had to remind myself of that later on. I fought off the desire just to go out and pick up someone and use him as a guinea pig for Karl's lessons. Lurking inside, though, was that old craving for a quick trick. I knew I had to teach myself not to use all these things I had set out to learn as gimmicks. I wanted to really expand my pleasure—and my knowledge.

31

I also needed to have the materials he'd talked about if I was going to do it the right way. So the next day I went shopping.

Finding the oils he'd mentioned was relatively easy. They were available in many different stores, just as he'd said they'd be. I found one package that contained a selection of three different massage oils. The fine print told me that they were edible. Why not choose them? I decided, just in case. . . . There was one bottle of almond, one of mint, and the third was coconut. That should be enough of a range to satisfy a variety of tastes.

The next stop was a little more difficult. I wanted to buy a vibrator like the one Karl had shown me. I had been to a number of adult sex stores in the city, checking out magazines, books, and videos and had noticed the large selection of dildos in the counters.

I walked into the largest one and studied their selection. They were all kept behind glass. Most of them looked like models of real cocks. I asked the clerk to take some out so I could see them. He acted as though I'd asked the strangest question he'd ever heard. "Most people just grab one they like the looks of," he growled.

"Well, not anymore," I answered. I wanted to know what I was going to use on my body these days. I suppose I always should have been this careful. It seemed like the health crisis was having its effect on other parts of my self-care as well. It might be a gain that was made at a lousy cost, but I wasn't going to argue with it.

The first dildo I picked up was an invitation to a major medical problem. It was made of hard plastic. I'm sure the clerk and the manufacturer would have claimed that it was too solid to break. But I wasn't about to experiment with this kind of dangerous toy.

Another one had a handle at the base. If you rotated it,

the center moved in a way that seemed to promise that you'd feel the motion inside your body. "What makes this operate?" I asked.

The clerk shrugged. "There must be a wire down the center of it."

I looked at the rubbery material it was made of and wondered just what was supposed to keep that wire from poking out of its case and into me?

There were some simple latex models of penises that would have served their purpose for me. But I wasn't after just a substitute for a cock. After what Karl had taught me, I was going to keep on looking until I found something that was really going to give me a good time in a safe way.

I realized that the adult stores weren't necessarily the best places for me. I went on down the street to a large hardware store I had passed before. That's where I hit pay dirt.

There was a whole selection of vibrators in the small-appliance department, all made by companies whose brand names I knew and trusted. I looked through the display and recognized the one that Karl, himself, had used on me. I picked it up and was ready to take it to the counter when I saw still another little machine.

The words *marital enhancement features* was fancy double talk for sex play, I knew. Picking up the packages and reading the descriptions, I decided this was something I wanted to look into. I bought both machines.

Back home, I unwrapped the two vibrators and set them out on the table by my bed. I stripped down and then took a long, warm bath. I wanted to replicate the relaxing effects of Karl's massage; I was trying to see if I could do as much for myself as his ministrations had done for me.

I dried off after the bath and then went into the bedroom. I sprawled naked on the sheet and picked up the wand vibrator. It was already plugged in and ready to go. I flicked the switch and the low, whirring sound began.

The controls allowed me to adjust the strength of the vibrations. I decided to start off on low. The wand machine has a round top to it where the actual motion is located. It's about two inches in diameter and no more than a half inch thick. The motion is so fast, and the area involved is so relatively small, that you can't actually see anything. But when you touch the tip to your body, you certainly can feel a lot.

I ran the edge of the disc over my shoulders and got that same good feeling. I let it move down over my chest and onto my hips. Sometimes, for instance, when it was working on a part of me where the bone was close to the surface of my body, the sensation wasn't as pleasurable as it could be. But it did eventually move to my penis. . . .

When I let the trembling, hard plastic touch the head of my cock, the response was immediate. My head had already sent out its messages that the whole of me was going to have a good time, so my body had already started getting ready for just that. When the vibrator began its work, though, the effect was immediate and concentrated.

I didn't want to be too clinical, but I watched the appliance as I ran it up and down the hardening shaft. It looked as though the glans was going to just burst from the attention when the disc traveled to the end of my cock and rested there on my glans.

I played with it—teasing myself by letting the intense stimulation on the head of my cock go on for as long as I could stand it but then removing it in time and, instead, letting the vibrator send its less extreme, but still good, sensations up and down the shaft.

Finally I turned the machine off. I was breathing deeply, a sure sign that I was *really* turned on. I looked down at my hard cock and had the urge just to grab it and wank it off. But I realized that this was as much a part of what I had to change as anything else.

Just as I would usually just go out and try to find a trick to fuck with in the old days, I was still trapped in the idea that masturbation was only a quick and furious exercise in orgasm. The trip to Karl's was meant to teach me some broader horizons. I needed to practice them on myself.

I reached over and took out the bottle of mint oil that was in the massage kit I'd gotten. I opened it and dabbed some on my hand, then used the oil to grease my cock. I rubbed my hand into my thighs afterward, being careful to use the same kinds of motions Karl had when he'd been massaging that part of my body.

There was still enough lubrication on my palm that I could glide it over my upper torso as well, running it over my chest and up and down my other arm. This wasn't aimed at getting me off quickly; it was supposed to make me more aware and more appreciative of my body. It was doing the job awfully well.

There were parts of me that were tingling by the time I was finished. There seemed to be something special in the mint oil that left my skin feeling extra cool. I blew down on my chest, and the air from my breath only made that sensation more intense.

I took up the other vibrator now. Instead of the long handle of the wand machine, this one fit easily into my hand. The vibrating element was a small nozzle at the end of a short protrusion in the spherical appliance. There was a series of different attachments that could be applied to that knob. These were those "marital aids" that the box had so discretely mentioned.

There were a couple that were clones of the wand vibrator's. I decided to try a couple of the others instead. They called one of them a "twig." The small, two-pronged element wasn't exactly trunklike, so I supposed the name was accurate enough.

There was a latex extension that stood out from the appliance at a ninety-degree angle. Off of it branched another, smaller length of latex. I had to study it for a minute to realize the purpose of the structure. If you used this on a woman, then you could insert the larger one, and the smaller one would provide a simultaneous external stimulation. That was an arrangement that a lot of women I knew would really like. I decided to keep that in mind for future reference.

There was a cuplike attachment that I couldn't figure out at first. It was called "the crown." Finally I figured out that it would just go around the head of a penis. That made sense. I chose that for the first part of the experiment.

I put it on the machine and turned the switch. I was ready to apply it to my cock when I realized that I was going back to just paying attention to my penis again. That wasn't supposed to be the agenda here. Then it dawned on me to use both machines at once. Why not?

I had them both switched on, and they were both whirring away. I carefully applied the crown around the top of my cock. It fit just right, acting like a little cap that the head could fit under. The vibrating was intense, and stimulation was amazing. It wasn't the same as a good blow job—but I wasn't looking for exact substitutes, I wanted alternatives. This was a choice I could be happy to make.

The other vibrator—the wand—I used to run up and down my thighs. I let it slip down between them. The disc touched my balls and sent a shiver through me. I moved it down into the area in the cleft of my buttocks, and as soon as the trembling struck my anus, I knew I had found a gold mine.

With the vibrating pieces of the apparatuses working on

my front and back, I felt that loss of control you get when you're having *dynamite* sex. There was this growing wave of my orgasm gripping hold of me. I could have removed the machines and regained myself, but I didn't want to. I'd done enough exploration for one session, I decided. I'd earned this reward.

The pressure built and built in my balls, and I knew that there wasn't going to be any way to keep myself from exploding into a powerful orgasm. I flicked the two vibrators off when I knew what was going to happen. It just came up on me, taking over of its own accord and sending the whole of my body into major spasms.

I lay on the bed panting at first. I had these fleeting memories of all the times I had just rolled over, often in annoyance, and "taken care" of an erection with a quick jack-off session. Now, with my skin tingling and with the scent of mint wafting over my body, I realized that this whole exploration of safe sex was going to mean even more changes in my life than I had realized.

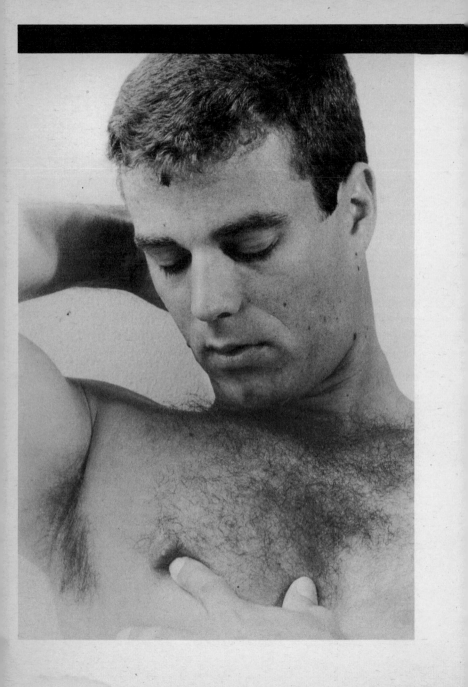

CHAPTER THREE

SOME PARTS EQUAL A WHOLE

"What are you up to these days, Glenn?"

Mike and I were in the shower room after a hard workout. I turned off the water and pushed my hands through my hair to get it back off my face.

The question was simple and honest, but I was having a hard time with the answer. There was no good reason for that. Mike was as savvy about gay life as anyone else I knew.

I also knew that in the old days Mike was one of the regulars in the cruise bars in Coconut Grove and Fort Lauderdale. He was hardly someone I had to hide my new interest in safe sex from. But I *was* embarrassed. It seemed a strange thing just to up and say that you were involved in safe sex.

I realized at that moment that talking about safe sex was going to have to be one of the things I spoke to other people about. We had to get over the idea that it was a weird or taboo topic. It had to be accepted as normal, as normal as any other kind of sexual consideration. In fact, it had to become even more commonplace.

"I, uh, I'm going to work as Mr. Safe Sex." I said, just leaving it at that.

Mike was actually very interested. "Tell me about it," he said. "What have you been up to with this stuff?"

I explained the offer I'd gotten and the first moves I'd made in exploring just what the options were. I didn't mind telling him about the experience at Karl's, but at first I had trouble talking about the visits to stores looking for vibrators.

Mike's enthusiasm made me forget that momentary shyness about the topic. As he and I went to our lockers he kept asking me what I'd learned about the various machines and how they could be used.

"You were damn smart not to get one of those plastic dildos," he said as he pulled on his jeans. "I know one guy who broke one while he had it inside him. When he came, his sphincter muscles clamped down hard and the thing shattered. He ended up with a very unpleasant trip to the emergency ward.

"You know"—he was smiling now—"your investigation of all these machines is fine. But you're overlooking some of your own natural resources for safe sex."

"What do you mean?"

We were both dressed now. We walked out into the hallway of the club. "Let's have a cool drink and I'll tell you about it," he said.

"Sure," I agreed. We went into the juice bar and ordered. When we had our drinks, he began to explain.

"You're on the right track when you talk about how much sex became something that was solely aimed at the cock and balls. Why think about anything else when there were so many places where you could go and someone would either get down on his knees and do you—or you could do him?

"The time of day didn't matter, and you weren't even in any trouble if you weren't downtown; there were plenty of places in the suburbs and on the beaches. You'd never have to do anything more than make some eye contact with a guy and . . . you were off to the races.

"It was just the times. So, since everything was so efficient, people only looked at the end result. They wanted to get off, and they did. They did it as often as they had the desire. It was well and good, if that's what people wanted. But there have always been those of us who were interested in other things."

I perked up when I heard that last statement. I wasn't sure what Mike was talking about. I knew that he was a guy who'd spent a lot of time in the bars, and I knew that the gossip said he was super sex, but I hadn't heard that he was into anything too bizarre.

"What are these 'other things' you're talking about?" I asked.

"There are lots of us who have a particular interest in parts of the body besides just our cocks and asses, that's all. Some of us have made our fascinations something of a specialty. I think it's stuff that you should know about, Glenn. It fits right into what you're doing."

"How do you mean?"

"Well," he said with that big, boyish smile, "I think we're talking about something that's best demonstrated rather than lectured about. How about coming back to my place and I'll show you the wonders of some parts of your body that I'm sure you neglect?"

"In the interest of science?" I asked.

"Of course," he answered, smiling even more now.

We went back to his apartment. I'd never been there; I wasn't sure why. I realized that it might have had something to do with having known him fairly well from the gym. It seemed as though sometimes, when you knew a guy too well, there wasn't the mystery in it that tricking could have. Well, that was another thing that was going to be changing, I realized.

There would have to be a lot more sex with buddies if I was going to continue with the safe-sex program. It just made more sense to be able to eroticize your friends and have sexual experiences with them. Besides, if *I* practiced safe sex with everyone, then I wasn't likely to be exposed to anything. But that didn't mean that it wasn't good to be able to know what was going on with the health of your partners.

At Mike's place I felt a little awkward. It was a fine apartment, very masculine in the way it was furnished. Only a few framed posters covered the wall, and a collection of very large pillows in a corner obviously substituted for other, more complicated furniture. There was a bed, a desk, a table, and some chairs for eating. A set of weights finished it off, obviously for those days when he didn't get to the gym for a full workout.

There were some books lined up in a bookcase on one of the walls. I looked them over while Mike went about taking care of a few things. When he was done, he brought back a couple glasses of mineral water, handing one to me. Then he sat down on a heap of the pillows and patted the ones next to him as an invitation for me to join him.

We chatted about the gym and other topics, all but the one that had brought us together. The conversation distracted me. With him right beside me I wasn't able to put off the awareness that we were going to be doing some sexual experimentation.

I wasn't particularly nervous. That wasn't the issue. Instead, I was simply more aware of his body than I think I had ever been before. I had seen him in the shower, on the floor, and in the locker room countless times. When you've been with someone and you've both been so naked, or close to it, so often, you'd think that the erotic potential would have been something that would have been obvious. But I realized now that that wasn't the case at all.

I wondered how much it had to do with that idea of not

thinking of buddies as sex partners. I don't have any great theories about it, but it must be easier to make some stranger into your fantasy than to deal with the reality of guys who are right there with you and whose characteristics you can study up close.

Was that what led so many men into anonymous sex? That we didn't know how to deal with the sexual potential of the people who are parts of our lives? I felt no little amount of discomfort sitting and talking to Mike and knowing that we were going to have sex—there was no doubt about that. I wasn't sure what the cause was, though. Was I frightened that he'd discover some previously unknown thing about me and tell all our mutual acquaintances? Was there something more difficult about the idea that someone you knew well would reject you than the little hurt you got when a stranger in a bar walked away full of his own attitude?

At least I was finding some questions that I knew people were going to be asking, even if I didn't know the answers to any of them yet.

"Well, are you interested in learning about my deep, dark secrets?" Mike finally asked.

"Are they that deep and dark?" I teased him.

"Oh, no. Not at all. I've discovered they're very common, in fact. Some of them, at least. I should explain more. Glenn, I'm sure you know my reputation. I'm really into sex, there's no doubt about it. For years and years I would get into just about any kind of thing you can think of, but it wasn't always satisfying in itself. As you get older, well, you realize there are fewer reasons to avoid being honest. . . ."

"Mike, for someone who claims he doesn't have a deep, dark secret, you sure aren't being very straightforward," I said.

"Yeah, it would be easier in the back room of a bar to have something happen. I used to let guys just fool around any way they wanted to, and when they did the 'right' thing, I'd let them know exactly how pleased I was, by talking dirty to them or else by groaning all the harder.

"You see, they would be going at my cock or my ass, which was fine. But they were never going to get me off until they started playing with my nipples.

"I'd be embarrassed about it. It didn't seem right that a guy would want to have his tits played with as much as I did. But I learned that there are more and more men like me who think of their nipples as being just as important as their cocks or their balls."

"That's your secret?" It certainly didn't sound too strange to me. I had much more complex images floating around my head of what Mike was going to want to get into than that.

"That's it." He sat up, put down his glass, and then pulled off his T-shirt.

Mike's body isn't one of the huge ones that you often see in a gymnasium. He'd always worked for definition rather than bulk. That earlier, silent question of mine about how and when we think of people in terms of their erotic potential came back to me now as I sat beside him. He only had his jeans on now. I was close enough to smell the odor of his soap from the shower mixed with just a tinge of his sweat from the warm day.

The simple statement he'd made about his nipples changed the way I was perceiving him, all right. I immediately stared down at his chest. I had known that he'd worked on it more than he did the rest of his body. His regular workout had left him with a trim waist; good, solid legs; a firm ass; and tight arm muscles. But his special emphasis had led to a much more developed set of pectoral muscles. They were almost out of proportion to the rest of him.

I was still studying them, feeling a response to the smooth skin and the rounded lines that defined the chest, when he did the most sensual thing I could imagine. Both his hands reached up to let his fingers gently touch each of his nipples. He flicked them, ever so slightly, using very quick, repeated motions.

He stopped for a moment to wet his fingers with his tongue. Then he went back to his chest. He was obviously exciting himself. I could see that from the growing bulge in his pants.

He looked up at me and smiled. "This is it. Let me show you how good it can be."

I didn't resist when he reached over and unbuttoned my shirt. He pulled it open and leaned over. I knew he was going to start using his mouth. Now, having someone lick and suck on my nipples was something that I'd found pleasurable enough before. But I wasn't prepared for Mike's expertise.

He began by using his tongue to flick over the surface of one of my tits, just as he had used his fingers on his own. The effect was like teasing, egging me on with the idea of his hot, wet tongue paying such close attention to one part of my body.

Another time I might have thought that this was a teasing prelude to something else. But I understood that this was probably the main act with Mike. This was what we were going to be doing. I sank back into the pillow and wondered if it really could be satisfying enough for him to go on and on with it.

There was no doubt that it was satisfying to me. I realized that a part of it was simply receiving so very much attention. I flashed on the idea that it was the same with the encounter with Karl: These guys were totally focused on giving me pleasure. There was always the possibility of reciprocation, but that would come later. I was only being asked to lay back and enjoy for the time being.

Mike shifted his body a bit. I let my hand closest to him rest on his body. The nearly hairless stomach and side were soft, the firm muscle underneath the taut skin warm and inviting. I just moved my hand gently, in small circles, to feel that part of him.

He had taken advantage of his new position and had reached up one of his own hands to gently pinch my other nipple. The new sensation, added to the ongoing movement of his tongue, was getting to me. It seemed as though my nipples were actually growing. I knew that the small pieces of brownish flesh were erectile tissue—just like a tiny cock, they grew when they were aroused. Now, with so much directed right at them and my mind forced to focus on them, I could sense them hardening in response to Mike's attention.

My cock was also hard and fighting against the restraints of my shorts. I wanted to reach down and take it out—that old urge just to jerk off fast as soon as I was turned on was getting to me again. But this was a *lesson*, I tried to remind myself. I giggled a little bit, thinking maybe I should take notes.

Mike looked up at me. "Anything wrong?"

"Not at all!" I said. I put my free hand on his neck and guided him back down onto the tit that suddenly felt so cold and naked after he'd taken his mouth away from it. I was telling the truth. The action was wonderful and a turn-on.

He moved his body again, shifting his lips from one side of my chest to the other. I realized that the first nipple had become very sensitive after all the oral attention it'd received. When he began to play with it, with his hand now, it was much more responsive than I had known it to be. The slightest motions of his fingers sent small little messages in a straight line down to my crotch.

I couldn't help from starting to let him know about my reactions. The constant erotic sensations bombarding my chest were taking away any ability—or desire—of maintaining a cool facade. I began to squirm. This was incredible pleasure.

But he wasn't about to let up. He would move back and forth, from one nipple to the other. I was left just making my

little moaning sounds and running my hand over his handsome body. He had positioned himself so I couldn't have
reached down to my cock if I wanted to. It just would have
to keep the faith and wait, hot and hard as it might be.

Maybe the best way for me to handle my excitement now
was to try to begin reciprocating, I decided. If I had the
excitement of his body as a part of my own physical experience, then I might be able to handle the intense stimulation
a little bit better.

The hand I had left on his side started to roam now. I
undid the buckle of his jeans and slipped down inside them.
My palm was resting over the elastic cup of his jockstrap. I
could easily feel his hard erection and the tightened testicles
underneath the clinging fabric. I could tell he liked the
contact; he gave an immediate response with the pressure he
was applying to my nipples. For once, he was the one who
was letting out the little moan.

Still, as much as I liked the feel of his cock and balls, I had
been given a very clear message about what would really get
to him. I brought my hand up out of the warm, damp crotch,
and moving it up over the hard belly again, I found one of
his nipples.

I had already seen that his tits were more pronounced
than mine. He must have been working on them a lot. They
were darker in color than mine, I also remembered. That
had been all the more apparent since, unlike me, he was
blond—I was dark and had more chest hair.

As soon as I touched one nipple Mike began to get more
agitated. While my whole mind was centered on the constant and erotic attention he was giving my tits, he had been
going without any stimulation there at all until now—and
that was really what he wanted the most. Finally receiving
his gratification obviously was turning him on.

I rolled the hard bit of flesh between two of my fingers. I

liked the way he reacted with all of his body. I could see the lines of his muscles become more pronounced as he breathed more deeply and moved around with that same lack of control I had felt before.

More than ever I wanted just to get on with it now. I wanted to roll him over, pull his pants all the way down, and just start a good, hot sixty-nine session going.

Bingo! From the mouths of babes . . . sixty-nine was just what was called for. But the new version, maestro. No diving for hard cocks and racing to the climax for Mr. Safe Sex. We'd have to begin some redefinitions right here and now.

I was the one who started moving. Mike was obviously not sure what I was up to, but he wasn't going to fight me. He kept his mouth on my one nipple and his hand on the other, letting me rearrange his body over the heap of pillows.

When he was on his back, my chest still attached to his suctioning lips, I leaned down and was able to take one of his own tits into my mouth. He groaned deeply now—some dream of his was coming true. He involuntarily lifted up his hips, and I could see that the pressure on his elastic jockstrap was getting close to a critical point.

I was able to easily rest my body on my knees and elbows and have enough maneuvering room so that my mouth could do its own wandering over his smooth, handsome chest. I would follow his more expert lead as to what kinds of stimulation to provide. Sometimes I would use the edge of my teeth to nip at his erect nipples. Other times I would just have my tonuge move lightly over the surface. Occasionally we'd both suck hard on the hungry little pieces of skin.

It seemed as though we were making actual connections between ourselves now. As much as I had loved being the passive recipient of all that pleasure, I was enjoying this even more. There was electricity between us as we'd move and alter the stimulation we were giving and getting. My hair chest was pressed against his face; my mouth was glued to his pectorals.

The sensations went on and on for a long time, but there was no denying the building need that we were both feeling. The motions of his pelvis were becoming more dramatic, and I understood just what was driving them. I thought my own cock was going to break out of my skin.

We changed positions again, now on our sides. The pillows gave us good enough leverage that we were able to maintain our energetic tit-play while I was able to reach his hard cock.

Now, understand, just because I was trying to get away from the idea of *only* being interested in erections and orgasms, that has never meant that I was ignoring them completely. Hey, come on! This was to make sex better, not to eliminate it.

Mike was just as understanding as I was trying to be. I felt his hand move into my shorts and underneath my jock to get my erection. We began to move with one another, letting our bodies help our hands apply steady streams of motion to arouse us. With all the foreplay that we'd engaged in with our tits, we'd made our cocks wait their turn, and they were anxious to make up for lost time.

I could feel Mike's balls lift up and pull themselves against his body. That was a sure sign that he was getting ready. My own were doing the same thing. Then I felt the undeniable signal that his cock was going to shoot: The hard flesh began to pulse just before there was a loud and primal growl from Mike. Then the cum shot out on to my hand.

I felt myself getting closer and closer and then . . .

When he'd caught his breath, Mike smiled at me, "Hey, Mr. Safe Sex, I don't think your lesson's done."

"Oh, come on," I protested. "I can't go another round of that now!"

"No, no, that's not what I meant. You have to learn to prolong the sensual part of sex in all ways, though. How about a nice, long shower together. You wash my back, I'll wash yours? Maybe a few other things as well."

"You're on."

We jumped into his shower and let the water roll off us. We kept our promises and scrubbed each other's back, though I have to admit that we seemed to pay more attention to the lower regions than to the shoulders. There was something especially sexual about being able to touch and feel a man without the pressures of orgasm. I realized I appreciated this little time with Mike. I'd done some hot things in shower stalls before, but I hadn't taken the time to do the slow and careful explorations that we were engaged in this time.

I suppose it was something close to what another friend called the "most honest moments of life"—the few minutes after sex when you stay there on a bed and hold each other, keeping the threads of intimacy intact before the realities of daily life come in on you and you have to go back to the real world (or before you might tell little lies about seeing one another again).

It seemed to me, while Mike and I playfully lathered each other up and carefully felt each other's bodies, that part of the safe-sex agenda had to be making those "most honest moments of life" extend a lot longer.

There was one moment when we stood there and had each other's testicles in our hands. We were kissing, but the idea that we had a hold on our balls was more impressive all of a sudden, and not in a sexual way this time. I mean, Jesus, how much more trust can two guys show than to touch each other this way?

When we finally had to get out of the shower, we dried each other off and went back into the living room.

We didn't get dressed again right away, which was fine by

me. I liked watching the handsome body on the guy as he moved around, put on some low music, and made some tea. While we were drinking it he told me that I'd find a lot of people who had made "specialties" of specific parts of their bodies. They certainly weren't limited to nipples. There were guys who were into feet, hands, you name it.

In the past they might have felt strange, just as Mike said he used to feel embarrassed by his proclivity. But now, with the need to expand the limits of our sexuality, the idea of mining what some other people called "fetishes" was one thing that I could teach people.

"Look, you had a good time, right? But you weren't someone who *knew* that this was his thing. Still, you can get into it, you understand that now. So you can use this to make sure that your sexual encounters are the highest quality you could want. Remember that, Glenn, it's something you can teach people about. The various parts of their bodies—in addition to the ones they're all aware of—can hold unexpected treasures if they'll just get into them."

We sat awhile and I took it all in. I knew he was right. Remembering the way Karl had made my feet feel, I realized it was a lot simpler than I'd thought. When Mike talked about people who could make a fetish out of that, well, I was pretty sure I'd be looking out for that treatment.

But I was more worried about something else right then. I couldn't help but realize that I was aware that Mike and I were both naked. I'd even had trouble taking off my clothes in Karl's studio. But I was going to become Mr. Safe Sex. I was going to have to get over this hassle with going around nude.

That was obviously the next lesson I'd have to learn.

CHAPTER FOUR

TIME FOR SHOW AND TELL

"Glenn, I have a hard time believing you need my advice on how to take off your clothes."

"Come on, Professor, you have to take me seriously."

I called Larry "Professor" because he taught drama at a local college. Actually he was about my age and didn't look the part at all. He was an avid tennis player with reddish hair, the highlights brought out by all that time on the courts—which had also left him with a deep tan.

I had come to him on other occasions, when I needed help in my nonerotic acting, and he'd been good about coaching me. But I suppose my most recent request wasn't the kind he was used to getting from his students in the classroom or out of it.

"But, Glenn, you've taken off *all* your clothes in movies; you've been photographed nude for magazines . . ."

"But this is different. Don't you realize what those times were like?"

"I've never indulged in your own arena of success," he said with a smirk. Larry was one of the best classical actors and directors in the area. My excursions into erotic films and pictures weren't exactly his cup of tea, and we'd never really talked about them before. Our conversations usually involved my plans for a "straight" acting career.

"Larry, do you know what the set of an erotic film is like?"

"Are you going to disillusion me?"

"I'm afraid so. I know that everyone thinks that it's something wonderful, all kinds of hot and horny hunks wandering around with ever-hard dicks, raring to go, doing it so fast that the cameramen have to run like hell to keep up with it all . . ."

"And it isn't so?"

"Maybe for the first half hour the first time you do it," I explained. "After that it's all work and so little play that you have a terrible time being able to keep up with it. You're standing there, waiting for your cue, watching the two leads getting it on, and all you can think is, 'If he doesn't climax soon, I'm going to miss my coffee break.'

"Doing a photo shoot is only a little better. You're there with a photographer, maybe a technical assistant or two, perhaps another model. But everything's in the posing, and you have to worry about it so much that you quickly lose track of anything else."

"Glenn, you're talking about my deepest fantasies here—and you're ruining them. It's not funny."

"You're damn right it's not. It's very difficult work, and it's usually boring. But it has nothing to do with this. Look, I'm not just going to have to get up on stage and take off my clothes. That would be one thing; I'm pretty sure I could handle it. I have to be able to do it in a way that people can do themselves. The whole point is to give the guys something they can walk out of the theater with. They're going to have to be able to take this home and use it."

"You want to produce a whole generation of Total Homosexuals, is that it?" He laughed, then scoffed at my expression. "Don't take everything I say so seriously, Glenn. Let's talk over what you really need to accomplish, and then we'll see if I can help you out."

"First of all," I began, thankful that Larry was finally treating my concerns more seriously, "I have to be able to get this message to them. I have to get them to listen to what I have to say."

"Well, you're going to have to begin with a strong persona, then. I should imagine your Marine image is the one for that."

"Yeah, I thought so. But then, I also want to be able to make it erotic. They can hear the words lots of places. But I have to make it into something that's so hot, they'll believe that they can take it home and use it."

"That's where the hard part comes. I can help you with the message part of your act fairly easily. The other is one of the more difficult assignments that any actor—or, for that matter, director—ever receives. Actually, when people are asked to take off their clothes on the stage, their usual concerns are quite the opposite of yours. The actor worries about an erection, or else thinks that his being unclothed will overshadow the lines he's trying to deliver because the audience will only be interested in the display of nudity. But you *want* to be taken as a sexual object by these men."

"That's how I'm going to reach them."

"Well, you're going to have to learn to be a fabulous stripper, then."

"That's it exactly. But just because I've taken off my clothes before doesn't mean I know how to do it well."

"I wonder, Glenn, if we're not really examining more of your own personal psychology than you realize."

"What do you mean?"

"Given your choices of occupation, I'd say you were a little bit more than a slight exhibitionist."

"Yeah, well . . ."

"Don't be embarrassed. Isn't that what this is all about? Aren't you trying to find some of the ways that people enjoy themselves sexually that aren't health dangers and not only give them permission to indulge in those tastes but also help them do it better? In ways that will give both them and their partners more enjoyment?"

I had to admit that his rationale sounded pretty good. "Yes. That's what I mean."

"Then, what you, yourself, are trying to do is take this element of your own sexuality, your enjoyment of other people watching you, and enjoy it more. I think we should treat this not as a performance piece, but as something that you are doing on your own accord for your own personal uses."

"You're starting to sound like that director in *A Chorus Line,* who put the dancers auditioning for his show through all those psychological exercises."

"I promise you, there aren't many drama teachers who get requests for this kind of training."

Larry still seemed awfully smug about it. I had to admit that maybe he was doing it on purpose. He went and sat down in a large easy chair in his living room, folding his arms across his chest. "Now, let's see you take off your clothes in a way that will satisfy my desires."

Just like that. My body went rigid as all the Marine in me came back. My spine straightened up. I tried to will myself to relax, but I wasn't able to. I put my hands on the top button of my shirt . . .

"Wait, you act like you're in some kind of corner Laundromat," Larry interrupted. "You're with a lover; a potential sex

partner, at least. You're trying to seduce him. Isn't the lack
of seduction part of what you're saying is missing?

"This is your starring role, Glenn. You have the most
important audience of the moment in front of you. The least
you can do is use your eyes on him."

I smirked at that one. I've been known to give people a
certain . . . look when I wanted to get my way. I remembered how it worked. I dipped my head down, so I had to
move my eyes a little bit when I stared at him.

"Good, good, now move your head just a bit to the side,
create a bit of an angle. That's it . . ."

Now, when my hand moved to the top button again, I
knew I was in much better shape. I was on home ground. I
remembered other parts of the training. The one message
that obviously was going to be coming through loud and
clear in this thing was simple: Go slow.

I moved down to the next button, then the third. I let my
fingers just sort of fall from one to the next. When I got to
my waist, I slowly lifted up the tails, dragging them out from
under the belt.

Larry was right. I do like to have people watch me. I just
had never been in a place where I was able to have them do
it in this sensual way. I'd gotten used to being stared at in
the bars and at the gym and by the swimming pool, but
there weren't many times when the very idea of people
staring at me had been sexual for me. But I was enjoying
this—a lot.

I pulled back the shirt now, revealing my chest. I'd worked
hard at the weights and the machines to get this part of my
body in shape, and I was happy to show it off. Looking at
Larry the first time, I rubbed my chest.

The drama professor was paying close attention to me. I
wondered if he was really getting off on just the idea of my

undressing in front of him or if he was still being a distant professional.

But the concern about what he was thinking wasn't so great anymore. I was into the idea of displaying myself. My hand roamed downward over my belly. I'd been working awfully hard on it recently, and I liked being able to sense that it was firm and tight.

Larry seemed to squirm in his seat a little bit.

I kicked off my loafers. I had on white athletic socks. I was happy about that. I like the look of those on my feet—with nothing else on. It might be fine to have just those on—good thing I'd chosen them.

I was getting an idea of my own now. I decided that the eye contact was something that we could lose for a minute. I turned around, my back to Larry. Unbuckling my belt, I slowly lowered the fly on my slacks, making sure he could hear the sound of the zipper as it moved. The slight noise of the metal moving against metal was a tease, and he had to know it.

Then I put my thumbs in the side of my slacks, using them to hold the pants up as much as anything else. There was nothing keeping them at my waist, but I wanted to know that I had Larry watching me carefully and thoroughly. I let the top of the slacks move down very, very deliberately. I was picturing him watching. I could just imagine what he was thinking. My ass was one of my better attributes; I'd gotten more than a few compliments on it.

Here it is, Larry, I thought to myself as I felt the cloth slipping down. I was almost totally exposed to him. I dropped my pants and left them in a pile on the floor.

That's when I turned around. I had on only a pair of brief underpants. Larry was right: I was turned on by the idea of stripping for someone this way. My cock was hard inside the cotton, and there was enough of a mound that it was per-fectly obvious to him—as it would have been to anyone else.

When I did turn around, I saw that Larry was into this whole little lesson even more than I had expected. His hands had moved down onto his lap. He was very subtly fondling himself. When our eyes met this time, I could actually see him gulp.

He nodded, as though to tell me to continue. Now that I understood just how much we were doing this together, I was able to make it all even more sexual than before.

I put the palm of my hand on my belly. I let it move down until it met the top of the underwear. Then I slipped my hand into the pouch and felt the hot and hard erection waiting for me.

I wanted to play with him, let him know that I was getting off on his watching me. I didn't take out my cock. Instead I let my hand grab hold of it, and I began to move my grip up and down its length.

For a while I was just interested in myself and the sensa-tion of doing something daring—so calmly jerking off in front of another man. But pretty soon I looked back at him. He was moving with me. His clothes were still on, but his hand was being much more obvious as it moved against his crotch.

There was something very exciting about the whole exhi-bition. I could feel it all over my body, not just in my cock. I reached up with my free hand and took hold of one of my nipples, still sensitive from the recent session with Mike. The visceral reaction to the mental turn-on and the physical stimulation was so intense that I threw my head back.

"No, no," Larry said in a soft voice. "Don't come yet. Let's do this right."

He stood up and went to the stereo. He put on a slow and emotional piece of classical music that I vaguely recognized. I could move with it, at least. He went back to his chair. Any idea that he was a distant teacher was gone. He took out his own cock.

I stared at it as it rose up out of his pants. It was nice and thick. I got a jolt of pleasure out of the idea that I had caused it to get hard like that. I smiled at him, more lewdly than before. This was getting funky. It wasn't just playacting anymore.

I could sense my mind working in different ways now. I could just imagine my talking to him. "Like what you see?"

I had on only the underpants and the socks now. The small pieces of cloth were all that kept me from being nude. But they actually made me feel more naked than I would have without them. They were tight reminders that those were the only small areas of my body where I was covered. The rest of me was open to his inspection.

I moved my hips slowly to the music. He seemed to be moving his hand on his cock in synchrony with me. I liked the idea of the lustfulness of it all. This was stripping for the sake of sex. This wasn't any minor prelude. We were doing the thing just this way, right here and now.

I actually think my cock got harder and bigger—at least, it felt that way as I continued to play with it under the cover of my underwear. I started to tease Larry a bit more. I'd let the top of my cock peak up over the band. I'd leave it there while I reached farther down and took hold of my balls.

"You like showing off that way, don't you?" Larry asked. There was a husky tone to his voice that let me know the scene was really getting to him. I wondered how long it would be before he came. I got a flush of pride and sexiness that just the sight of me was what could make him so horny.

"Yeah," I said, surprising myself with my own voice. "I like it a lot. I have a good body, work hard at it . . ."

"You have that, and you have a sexy personality; you project that. You like having someone watch you."

The music seemed to pick up tempo a bit. I was only vaguely aware that I was moving my hand faster on my cock. "You think I'm sexy?"

"Of course I do." Larry was starting to masturbate faster now. "I love being here and having a man like you stripping down for me, just for me. . . ."

"That's what it is, guy. It's happening just for you." I was staring at him directly now. I knew my expression was looking more stern. This was hard sex, good hot sex. We were looking right at each another now. It also seemed as though we were using the music to make sure our hands worked together. We were coming closer and closer to our climax.

I pushed down the edge of the underwear so that the band was caught underneath my testicles. My balls and hard cock were visible now. He was staring at them. I had this wild response to knowing that some man was looking at that part of my body with such obvious desire.

The music started going faster, and so did we. My mind was reeling about with all different kinds of images. I was getting off on at least a dozen things at once. There was the idea of standing naked and hard in front of him—that was the biggest part of it. But there was the image of him as well, sitting there with his clothes on and only his cock out. It was . . . dirty, in a way. I suddenly realized that the funk didn't have to be limited to back-room bars—you could get down in a guy's living room, too, if you just put your mind to it.

What else? I was getting off on my being a little bit dirty too. I was heaving my hips around, letting my pelvis do a number with the beat of the music. It felt wonderful to be so abandoned. This was some kind of extension of the same sensation I'd had of being naked with Mike but much, much more intense.

The music wasn't going to slow down—and I wasn't in any mood to, either. I could feel the skin in my scrotum tighten up, and it seemed like my cock was starting to pump even before there was any liquid shooting up out of it. But that, of course, was only a matter of time. . . .

Larry came at the same moment I did. "I don't like making that a major element in sex of any kind," he said.

"What do you mean?"

"The idea that you have *got* to have an orgasm at exactly the same time. In fact, it's one of those tyrannies of life that people insist you have to have one every time you have sex. It's nonsense. You should put that into your lecture, that people can often enjoy themselves without the concern of performance."

"Well, it seems like performance was the whole issue that time, Professor." We were sitting on his couch together now. He put a warm hand on my neck when I put my head on his shoulder.

"Of course, that's true. But the fact remains that there are plenty of times when two people can have wonderful sex and not have to prove it with an orgasm. Too often they turn coming into some kind of trophy. Unnecessary."

I leaned up and gave him a peck on the chin. "What about my act?"

"Glenn, your act will do just fine. You've uncovered one of the secrets of good drama: You have found something in yourself that you can use to project a character. When you start your act, just remember this little incident and think about the idea that you're not on a stage with a whole audience in front of you but just in this room with me, doing it with one guy."

"To tell you the truth," I said, "I might like the idea of a whole audience watching me."

"Then you'll be fine. But if you lose your nerve just think

back to today and you'll realize that you can draw on it. You shouldn't just get into the whole audience every time, anyway, or you might lose some of the power of your intimate reactions. The best thing to do is to try to pick out one man and play to him, just the way you did to me.

"Every man in the audience can think that he's the one you've chosen. It will thrill each man even more. If you act as though your stripping is a public event, you'll lose some of your impact. Much better to work on the stuff inside you that says, 'This is private, perhaps a little secret.' "

"What am I going to tell them about themselves?" I said. "I want them to walk out thinking there's something they can use."

"What thoughts were you having while it was going on? Maybe there's a key in those."

Suddenly I didn't like the turn the conversation was taking. Feeling uncomfortable, I pulled away from him, sitting with my arms resting on my knees. It was, I realized, the reaction of a real jock.

"Come on, Glenn, don't hold back your feelings. You're trying to get into some kind of elemental sex education here. Both as an educator and as an actor on a public stage, you are going to have to take away more than articles of clothing."

"Well, it felt . . . lewd. It felt like I was doing something indecent somehow."

"But you, yourself, said you undress in front of other people a lot."

"Yeah, but this was for the express purpose of turning someone on."

"What are you saying? That it was bad? That you feel guilty?"

"Well, I think it was *hot*. I know it was difficult for me to get over the idea of acting that way in front of you. Other guys are going to have that problem too.

"They're going to have to do it with people they have enough confidence in that they won't feel like fools. Not that they should—it's not anything they should feel bad about. I've gotta admit, it's dynamite to do it. Any guy who can get into this, throw his hips around, jut out his cock, all of it, even show off his ass will have one answer to the problem everyone's always complaining about: That sex is too boring if it's safe.

"But tell me something, Larry. Why was this so exciting to you? You got off on watching as much as I got off on doing the acting."

Larry had to think about that one for a minute. "It's like other things you've said, about the restraint we have to undergo during the sex crisis. You know, being in theater, I'm always aware of body movement; it's a large part of our training. But I approach it as you'd expect: as a professional.

"I realize when you started out here today that I could simply take it in the cool and analytic manner that I'm used to. I could have sat back and watched you, critiquing your performance and so on. Or I could, instead, choose to examine the other dimensions of what was going on. I could take something that I could—as I usually do—enjoy or criticize as a performance, or I could allow my fantasies to melt into your actions.

"As a drama person, I have always loved the idea of performances just for myself. This was a chance for me to get into some of my own personal fantasies about men in other situations which I wished had been overtly sexual, men whom I'd only been able to look at from a distance. I could take those other experiences in drama and transpose them to this afternoon.

"I'll tell you one thing: It's convinced me that you're right about safe sex. There are lots of ideas, fantasies, and arousals that we don't really take full advantage of; we keep them latent. It's time we stopped suppressing them.

"Watching you, I suddenly was reliving all these instances in my life that could have been turned into erotic adventures. But I hadn't allowed it to happen because I hadn't sensed the potential. That is what you're really going to be doing with people—I'm sure of it now. You're not going to take away the things they've liked and lusted after. Instead you're going to be leading them into other parts of their minds and help them discover erotic potentials they didn't even know existed.

"My own, here, this afternoon? My mind was all the places I've told you about—and more. You helped me take some of my unformed daydreams and turn them into much more complete erotic vehicles. I just know you'll be able to do it with other people as well. You're going to be expanding a great number of minds.

"Glenn, I just want you to know that you've only begun to explore the depths of theater in your work. I don't just mean in terms of what you might do on stage. You can also show people the acting that they can do in their own homes, with their friends and their lovers, that can help them create the performances of their lives."

CHAPTER FIVE

GETTING RUBBED THE RIGHT WAY

We all have one of them. It doesn't make any difference if you're a bodybuilder, a porn star, or a millionaire, there's still that one man who makes your stomach do loop-the-loops. He's the one who makes you wish you paid more attention to that mouthwash commercial on television or who you're *sure* is going to notice when you're looking less than your best.

For me that man is Zack.

Zack is not just handsome; he's the Most Handsome Man in Town. He doesn't have a good build; he has The Body.

I'd been spending a lot of time on the beach, and since I wanted to make sure I had a good tan, I would wear a very skimpy bathing suit. One day I was on the sand and I saw *him*. As soon as I realized that Zack was walking over to me, I had to roll over on my stomach. I wasn't at all sure the suit was big enough to contain the evidence of my reaction to him.

I tried not to be obvious. Actually, I didn't even know if he was going to come over to me. My infatuation for Zack was so instantaneous and so strong, in fact, that I think I overdid the cool act, almost hiding from him. For all I knew, he wasn't even aware that I knew he was alive. The thought that he might return my feelings was almost too scary to think about—it would make for major electricity, all right, but so much that it might cause a big electrical storm. The way I felt about Zack, if anything ever happened between us, it wasn't going to be limited to just a few sparks.

Here I was, a big, six-foot-two former Marine, but when Zack spoke to me, I turned into a blubbering adolescent. I remembered the last time we'd crossed paths on the beach: I had actually kicked the sand with my bare feet and said, "Shucks," in response to something he'd said.

It was that bad.

The last guy who'd made me feel this way was the captain of the football team in high school. With that guy, just like with Zack, I tried to prepare myself for rejection. I told myself that he'd just walk by me. Maybe he'd say hello, but that would be it.

When Zack actually did sit down beside me, I didn't know what to do. You'd think I'd be happy, but no. *Why's he doing this to me?* I thought.

"Glenn, how're you doing?"

I mumbled something in reply, thanking the good lord that I was wearing my dark sunglasses and wouldn't have to worry about him seeing my eyes and all they were revealing about my reaction to him.

"I heard your radio interview the other night when you were going into all that safe-sex stuff," he went on. "A guy at the gym said you were going on tour and everything."

The gym was the center of Zack's life. Mike and I were regulars, and we took care of our bodies, but Zack was devout in his commitment to his. The physical result was one of the reasons I—and most of the rest of the men in the state—were so taken by him.

There were many other justifications. There was the thick, dark brown hair and the matching mustache. The blue eyes didn't hurt—or the smile that revealed teeth that could be their own rationale for safe sex. (They were so perfect, you could imagine making love to them alone.)

He was shining them at me now. I finally got some intelligible words out. "Thanks, I'm sort of looking forward to it."

He turned to look out over the ocean. If I was momentarily relieved that he wasn't staring at me anymore, I realized I'd actually lost ground. Now I had to look at The Profile. It—like the rest of him—was perfect.

"It's been a hard haul," he said, still watching the surf break on the beach. "I guess I was like a lot of other guys. I decided I just wasn't ever going to have sex again."

Tragic!

"But I realized that couldn't work. I believe we should use the bodies we have, and we should have as much pleasure as possible with them."

Thank God!

"But I just couldn't get past losing some things. The idea that I'd never get fucked again was awfully hard to face."

You like getting fucked? There must be a way. If there's a god in heaven, we'll find a way!

"I used to think that that was all sex was, really. I couldn't understand how it could be something worthwhile without that complete man-to-man experience."

"I've been getting into massage." I'm not even sure he heard me. My voice was so low that the words had a hard time getting out.

"Yeah, I tried that."

Let's do it! I thought. The image of Zack naked, on his

belly, with me rubbing those enormous muscles on his back, moving down . . .

"I know a lot of people are into it. I enjoy it but not as sex. Sex for me is something that has to be more energetic. I think that's what I used to love about fucking, really being able to feel someone, you know? I mean, I liked it when there was sweat and you had your whole body engaged in it with someone else. Do you understand?"

Did I understand! I made some sound that was supposed to be yes, but it came out like the noise a wounded animal would make. The bathing suit was getting smaller and smaller, and the sand underneath was getting harder and harder. . . .

"Yeah, those were the days."

Now, everything I was doing was a part of my new identity as Mr. Safe Sex. Here I was, listening to a person who was struggling with the new definitions of sexuality that we had to develop. I wanted to counsel him. The idea that I might have any ulterior motives should never enter into your mind.

"We can't look back, Zack. I think we have to learn how to work with what we have and make it as good as it can be."

"Oh, I agree," he said. He seemed a little surprised by my heartfelt statement. "I've learned a great deal about myself and my sexual tastes. God, I'm not celibate anymore."

"Oh?" My pulse picked up. *What?! What do you do now!? Can I do it with you?!*

"Sure, Glenn. You know, I should probably do stuff like you're doing. I could tell guys a thing or two about safe sex."

Want to give a demonstration?

"You know I'm in bodybuilding competition. I can turn that into an erotic act now—showing off."

I ran my tongue over a dry lip.

"I'm glad there are a lot of guys into that. I feel I can still turn them on and enjoy something hot with them. But you must know that. You get into that stuff yourself, don't you? I heard you did."

"Uh, yeah." I pictured us stripping down for one another. We could pull a mutual show, just like the one I'd done with Larry. Zack was wearing a bathing suit, not much larger than mine, topped by a tight T-shirt. I could already see most of his body. I imagined the two of us in a room alone and him slowly, slowly pulling down his briefs.

"But it doesn't work for me, either."

"What does?" I'm afraid I was yelling by now. I tried to regain my composure. "I mean . . . you said you don't get off enough on massage, and you're not really an exhibitionist. What *does* turn you on these days?" I got control of myself enough to realize that I needed a rationale for my explosion. "I'm trying to catalog the ways that guys are using safe sex, Zack. I need to ask people so I can incorporate their own solutions into my presentations."

"Oh, I understand." Zack was looking at me again. The Teeth were visible. I swear, if I hadn't been wearing sunglasses, the way the sun's rays bounced off the white enamel would have blinded me.

"I listened to what you said to the interviewer about needing to talk more about sex these days. I couldn't agree with you more. We should have been more open about these things all along. After all, we're grown men. We should be able to discuss any issue about ourselves without being embarrassed or uptight about it."

So, so! Come on. What are you into?

"I really just like to have a very physical experience, like I said. I like to get a big, muscular man and get into some wild times with him. I've discovered that there are plenty of ways it can happen without having to fuck." Then he did it. He turned on his biggest smile. Even through the sunglasses the reflection was dazzling. "Maybe we can just go back to my place and get into it. I don't mind talking—but I sure like 'doing' a lot more."

In addition to everything else, Zack is a gentleman. He never made a single remark about the way I held my towel in front of my bathing suit as we walked up the beach and onto the sidewalk. He lived in a high-rise close by, so luckily, I didn't have to concern myself with the subterfuge for long.

Zack had responded very positively to my comments about talking openly and honestly about sex. I was the one who kept avoiding all the real topics of conversation. I was still more than a bit in awe of my idol's response to me.

Finally I let go a slight smirk when I realized that getting into safe sex had resulted in some very real benefits. Zack and I had known each other for well over a year, and I'd been interested in him the whole time, but I'd been too in awe to make any kind of sexual approach. It was even worse than that: I hadn't even been able to talk to him intelligently. I'd always been tongue-tied.

But now, because I *had* talked about it on that radio show and was getting ready to speak to live audiences, *he* had approached *me*. I was going to have to include that in my rap: The more honest you are about sex, the more open you make yourself to other people being honest with you.

As soon as the door to his apartment closed behind us, Zack turned and took a firm hold on my arms. He pushed me back against the wall. I had put on my shirt, but it was unbuttoned. The pressure on my arms being splayed apart opened it, leaving my chest and belly naked.

He moved closer and pushed his body hard against mine. Our crotches rubbed against one another. I thought, for a quick moment, that he was trying to get into some kind of scene that I wasn't at all sure I wanted to be involved in.

Maybe I wasn't going to be ready for all the heavy action Larry had talked about when he mentioned my getting more involved in theatrics.

I was ready to say something to cool Zack off when he began to lift my arms up above my head. Suddenly I realized what he was really doing, and I stopped myself from interrupting.

As soon as my underarms were exposed, he bent his head into one and inhaled deeply. "Yeah," he said with a husky voice. He moved his head up and buried it in the crook of my neck. He rubbed his face in the fleshy junction of my arm and shoulder.

Then he backed off a bit, not letting go of my arms but moving himself away just enough to relieve the pressure and also to be able to look in my face. He was smiling with those teeth again. "Let's get naked."

I had originally thought we'd have a nice, easy chance to work up to sex. I had been learning to get off on the slow and mellow methods I'd been learning. I also had begun to equate sex with showers—at least baths. But Zack was definitely not interested. Oh, no. That was not his plan. We were going to get *down*.

He moved away from me now. He stood in the middle of the room and spread his legs far apart. His pose exaggerated The Crotch—if that was possible. He was grinning, but it wasn't one of his friendly, small-town-boy smiles. It had the edge of a sneer to it. He reached for the bottom hem of his shirt and pulled it up with a motion so quick and hard that I honestly thought it might rip.

There was The Chest. It began in the broad expanse of his shoulders and swooped downward and inward to the tight waist. The top of it was covered with a fan of dark body hair that funneled quickly into a trickle that ran over his belly, past his navel, and disappeared into his briefs.

I stood there and felt the heat in the apartment rise as something passed between us. I took my already open shirt and pulled it off, standing bare-chested as well. I kicked off my shoes and took off my socks. He had been wearing only sandals. They went flying across the room.

He moved over to me and took hold of the tops of my briefs. He yanked downward, forcing them over my hips and past my half-hard cock. "Like I said, let's get naked."

I caught the hint of a dare in his voice. I could sense more and more what he wanted. I put my own hands on the waist of his swimsuit and pulled it down. Now we both were able to step out of the clothing and stand close to one another. Our cocks were rising toward each other's and met in the small space that was left between our bodies.

He grabbed me around the middle and half led, half carried me over to the platform bed that dominated the other part of the big studio apartment. I was sprawled out on my back. He jumped on top of me, and his legs landed in between mine. As soon as he was able to get a footing, he used his beefy thighs to spread mine.

For a second I thought he was going to try to fuck me. I wasn't just surprised, I was angry. I started to fight him off, furious that he would pull that on me after I had been so clear about safe sex. But I realized that that wasn't what he was really after.

His cock was on top of my belly. His testicles were pressed against mine. He began to move his pelvis in forceful thrusts, but there was no attempt to lower his erection into position to enter me. This was exactly what he wanted.

And he wanted the resistance I was showing.

"That's right," he growled in a sexy voice, right into my ear, "let's wrestle for it."

I suddenly put all the pieces together: the talk about the man-to-man experience, the enjoyment of the odor of my body, the hints of combat. I thought I understood what Zack wanted now, and I wasn't in any mood to deny it.

We began to roll over the top of the platform bed. Our hard, naked bodies were pressed together, our chest hair getting soaked with sweat. The smells of two men were getting strong, and this only goaded us on. He would buck on top of me, seeming to lift himself and leaving only our midsections in contact with one another. My legs would lift up and wrap around him, my arms would grab his shoulders, and I'd force us back into flesh-on-flesh contact.

Suddenly he pulled back. He flashed a smile, and I could tell he wanted me to stay there for a second. He got up out of bed and I watched The Ass as he moved across the room to get something. He came back carrying a bottle of baby oil.

When he got to the edge of the bed, I was so hypnotized by The Cock that had been leading the way that I hardly noticed what he was doing with the oil. But there was a sudden stream cascading down over me. I jumped a little bit, remembering what Karl had said about ruining the mood of a massage with oil that was too cool. But this wasn't a soothing body rub we were going to get into.

Zack was having fun with the oil, watching it stream over me, making little circles with it up and down my belly, aiming it directly at my cock and balls. He was playing with this as though we were just a couple of college jocks having a good time. I still wasn't going to argue with him.

When he'd put so much on me that it had begun to form pools in the crevices of my muscles, he finally stopped. This time he moved slowly when he lowered his body on mine. He kissed me while he squirmed over me, using his own flesh to spread out the oil.

We started to slip and slide over one another. I moved and got him beneath me. My chest and thighs couldn't hold a position, though, and soon our bodies were writhing. The slick surfaces of our bodies kept us from staying in any one position for long.

First my arms would get a hold on something, and then he would be able to wriggle out of the position and move into another one. It was a little bit of wrestling with playful attempts to climb on top or to pin each other, but there wasn't any sense of combat.

Instead we both had a complete awareness of each other. I could feel all the parts of Zack's body that I'd seen—and worshiped—from a distance. His body hair was softer than I had imagined, more delicate than its thickness had led me to expect. The muscles were as firm as I had hoped, but as they always are, the feel of them wasn't as rock-hard as they looked. They were warm, firm, but not forbidding.

The exertion was incredible. Pretty soon we were panting from the effort. Our chests were heaving against one another, and our legs were wrapped together in such unusual positions that we'd inadvertently press too hard against our exposed and defenseless genitals.

One too-forceful move against his balls was all we needed to calm down a little. It was a good thing too; neither of us could have kept up that fever pitch of passion much longer.

We moved more slowly now. I was simply getting into the idea of having this idol in my arms. My hands stopped trying to grip him and instead started a slow and erotic exploration of his body. His reciprocated, examining mine. The kisses soon became the most important part of what we were doing.

Not that our pelvises stopped moving; they were going like demanding pistons. Our well-greased midsections kept pressing and pushing. My mind was carried away with the sensations of that wonderful contradiction of a man having sex: a hard erection balanced by totally vulnerable testicles.

I had been letting Zack take the lead. But now my hand moved down to his crotch and felt the satiny covering of his stiff penis and soft scrotum moving against my own. He let out a moan of pleasure.

But his constant motions let me know that he didn't want our hands to be providing the climax. That was all right with me. I took hold of his shoulders, spreading my palms out and letting them slip and slide up and down his body.

His shoulders were hard with muscle and bone, but I could delve down farther and feel the firm but spongy mass of his buttocks. I spread them apart, realizing that in another time I could have explored their hot and inviting center. That small prohibition seemed almost inconsequential now that I had The Body so close to me.

I rolled so that we were both on our sides. My arms were around his waist, and my hands were still able to reach down and grip his ass. He had no objection to what I was doing. I could move my head back a little bit now and see the physical beauty continuing to move in waves against me.

Zack was getting more and more excited. I could feel his cock become more demanding as it pressed against me. There was nothing but pleasure coming from the way we were bucking one another now.

Suddenly Zack reared back. "Get on your back," he said. He spoke more with an emphatic need than with any sense of a command. Obviously he wasn't going to be happy if I didn't comply. He lifted himself up with one arm and took his cock with the other, putting his hard erection between my thighs. "Close your legs," he ordered. I did, ensnaring his rigid flesh in mine.

He began to move with even more powerful thrusts of his hips. His cock glided in long, fast strokes between my legs. As he got closer and closer to climax, I could actually feel the way his cock was getting harder, more acutely than if he'd been fucking me.

Suddenly he arched his back. I was staring at The Chest as it began to heave. The orgasm took hold of him so completely that he almost seemed to come by hyperventilating. His entire upper torso seemed to expand and contract in nearly superhuman extremes.

Then he collapsed on top of me. I know that a lot of men just have to stop for a while after they come. But there are some who want to keep right on going. Thankfully Zack was one of the latter. He immediately rolled us over so that I was on top. He spread his legs and put my cock between them. Then, just as he'd had me do, he closed them around me.

My cock was caught by a fleshy trap that was as warm as anything my cock had been in before. The large amounts of oil had left it well lubricated. I began to follow his lead and to go through the same motions he had.

"Come on, come on," he began to whisper. His lips were right by my ear, and the soft sounds were urgent and compelling. I sped up, my cock moving against the slippery surface of his skin. Closer and closer to my own orgasm, I could feel it welling up in my balls as I continued the thrusting, letting my hard flesh move more and more quickly against him.

"Come on, stud, come on," he kept on whispering. "Shoot it all over me."

I could feel the beginning of release, and I lifted up quickly, as soon as I knew what he wanted. I wanted to see it myself.

I was just in time, with my belly over his, my now freed cock hard and parallel to his resting one. The pulsing waves of cum flowed out of me, spurting onto his stomach and up to his chest. The evidence of my satisfaction written on his body.

*   *   *

I stood in the living room getting dressed after my shower. As I pulled on my shirt I asked Zack if he didn't want to take one also.

The Body was spread out on top of the platform bed. For a minute I felt a little guilty about the oil stains on the covers— but that obviously wasn't something he was going to worry about.

"Later. I don't really mind letting myself enjoy all the little reminders of such a good time for a while," he said playfully. "Do you have to go so quickly?"

"Afraid so. I promised some people I'd meet them after I left the beach." The sun was beginning to go down now, and I did have to get together with some friends.

"Too bad. Want to come over again sometime soon?" The Teeth flashed at me.

"Sure," I got the words out somehow. "Yeah."

"For your act, so you can explain to people what this option's like?"

"Of course. Isn't that the only reason?" I was the one smiling now.

"It's a good one, Glenn. There are lots of variations, you know. We could have just plain wrestled. It can get pretty hot. Or we could make it into a more extravagant form of your massage trip. The thing is, guys don't have to give up that fierce part of our sexuality. There are still options if you want to get into being really masculine together."

"Macho safe sex, huh?"

He just smiled. I turned and went to open the door to leave.

"Hey, Glenn, you *are* coming back, aren't you?"

"Oh, yeah," I said. "I'll be coming back. Research."

"Got to get those particulars down."

"Every little detail, Zack. Every single little detail has to be laboratory-approved."

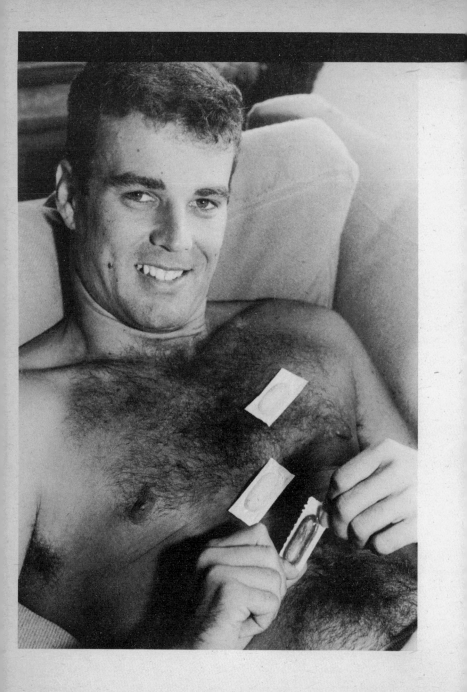

CHAPTER SIX

ALL NECESSARY PRECAUTIONS

There was something about the time with Zack that bugged me. I walked out of that apartment with a smile on my face, there was no doubt about that. But I realized one thing about discovering myself in the arms—and bed—of my idol. I realized that I would have been happy just to undress and cuddle with him.

Now, there's a part of safe sex that's worth talking about: just the idea of being close. I remember what Larry had said about the "tyranny of orgasm." When you're with someone you like *that* much, sexually or emotionally, then the act itself isn't necessarily as important as the idea of being close. Sex is the way we have of getting that closeness—but we don't always have to have hot and heavy fucking to go with it.

True—there was no way around it—hot and heavy fucking would still be nice.

But everything I'd read said that fucking was one of the most dangerous, and therefore, forbidden, things to do. There was an option, of course. The dreaded condom.

I'm not sure why I was so resentful of condoms. Some people say they're a bother, but it certainly seems like a whole lot of straight guys have been wearing them for an awfully long while and still seemed to have some hot times.

I've also heard some women talking about gay men's complaints about safe sex and responding—angrily—that they'd been having to deal with birth control from time immemorial and no one took their complaints seriously.

I also wonder about our complaints about condoms and their lack of sexiness. I certainly know that a lot of guys used to get off on them before the safe-sex need arose. They were little toys then, reminders of straight boys in high school. Those gay guys who were into it would make believe that using condoms with their partners reminded them of their classmates in high school. That seems like a fantasy about prophylactics that people should be able to get into.

But me? I still had trouble thinking about it.

Even when I'd been with women, who'd always asked responsible questions about birth control, my female partner had ended up taking control of it by the time we got together. As a result, I'd never had to deal with condoms.

Why were they such a hassle to me? For a lot of guys the passion of it all, the very fact that we didn't have to worry about the consequences, was part of the appeal of gay sex. Anything that made us slow down we found unwelcome. After the rules changed, some guys like Zack found the intensely masculine component of sex in new ways. I had experienced something pretty heavy myself with the hot and horny way I'd felt showing off for Larry. But lots of men weren't there yet.

It's easy to say: "Too bad, sucker. You have no choice," when people made complaints about the new restrictions on sexual activities. But when it came to having to wear condoms or not being able to fuck, I was one of those who was having a very difficult time of it.

I was embarrassed to realize that there was one particular problem I had: I didn't know how to use the things.

Now that might seem silly to you—even stupid. But I ask you, why should gay guys ever have to learn? It was embarrassing enough in high school if you were straight and had to discover how those strange things worked. It's even more awkward to be my age, my size, with my Marine/jock background, and to stand up in front of a guy and say, "I, uh, don't know how."

The fact that I was going to have to talk about condoms to my audiences was one of the most difficult ideas I had to face. I imagined myself going to a pharmacist and asking him to demonstrate for me. It was a humiliating idea. The fact that other people—straight men and women—had to do these things as a matter of course didn't make it any easier.

To be honest, a fear of condoms was a closet anxiety of mine while the plans for my first tour were being set up. Instead I threw myself into the rest of my preparations, leaving this supposedly unimportant element to linger, unresolved.

First order of the day was totally unrelated to "those things," or so I thought. I knew I was going to have to learn how to move on stage a lot more gracefully than I had in the few movies I'd been in, so I signed up with a dance coach I'd heard about. Don, the most highly regarded instructor in the area, had learned dance when he lived in New York and had performed with the best dance companies in Harlem and also on Broadway.

"Sure," he'd said when we first met, and I told him what I needed to learn. "I can take your movements and work you through them. But, Glenn, why not at least try to let me show you some exercises that will limber you up and make you more prepared for your stage performances? Also, there are some very basic movements you can learn now and use as a framework for some alterations in your act later on."

I explained my time limitations. I was going on the road soon and had my schedule at the gym to keep up.

"How much of that is just aerobics and running?" Don asked.

At least an hour a day was devoted to those activities, I told him.

He smiled. "My dance lessons are easily as good for you for the same purposes as running and most aerobics, if not more so. They'll also loosen you up a great deal more. I recommend an intensive course, five days a week, and I guarantee that you'll see marked improvement. What you're doing is important, Glenn, and I think you should do it right. You'll just have to learn a lot more about stage presence in the physical sense. I can teach you, if you give me the time and your concentration."

It seemed pretty serious, but I knew I was going to have to get my act together very quickly. I wanted it to be as good as possible. I knew myself—and Larry also had been adamant about this—that dance was something that would help me a lot.

Showing up for class in the morning, wearing dancers' tights and a dance belt instead of a jockstrap, confirmed my uneasiness about what I was doing. Still, it was just another thing that I had to get over, I knew.

Don turned out to be the hardest taskmaster I'd had since boot camp. It didn't help that he reminded me of Lou Gossett, Jr. in *An Officer and Gentleman*, either. I kept waiting for him to make me do push-ups when I fouled up some movement or something.

The warm-ups we started with were downright humiliating. I knew they were his version of getting me in touch with my body and its movement potential, but they weren't the gentle actions I'd learned from my experiences with massage. On the contrary, these squats and bends and leg lifts seemed to have been designed specifically to make me aware of how ungainly a man's big frame can be.

"Flow! More gracefully! Stop jerking your body!" Don would yell every day. There was no kind teacher here, just a real drill sergeant. The fact that he always had a canelike object in his hands didn't help, either. He'd use it to point out bad lines in my body or else to direct my other movements in one way or another. This must be the way guys who are into S&M must think of a dreaded whip, I thought. He never hit me, but the potential was always there.

I had to admit that he was doing me a lot of good. I could sense that my body was moving through space with something that, if not graceful, was at least not inept. In fact, I had to admit that over the weeks of my dance training I was growing to respect Don. He also seemed pleased with my progress, which meant a lot to me.

As time went by we became more friendly. I discovered that Don's willingness to give me lessons was very unusual for him. Although very much in demand as a teacher in our area, he'd made such an exception for me because he believed in what I was doing.

"I want you to go on the road in the best show possible," he said one day when we were having a cup of herbal tea after a lesson. "That's why I went out of my way to create the time for you."

Slowly, as our friendship became warmer, I began to look forward to the lessons more. And I began to look forward to seeing Don. This was all fitting into my new patterns of relating to people. I was consciously eroticizing men whom I might not have considered sexually before. With Don, a guy about my age with a terrific body, it didn't take long for a crush to start happening.

That made those dance exercises all the more intense. I would arrive in the tights that were sculpted to my legs and ass and begin the warm-up routines. I would be on the floor, sitting up with my legs out in front of me, doing stretches. I could feel the strap of the dance belt as it cut into the cleft of my butt. Then Don would walk into the room with the pointer in his hand. He'd stand in front of me and watch me as I worked.

When I stood up and went to the barre, he'd move with me. It seemed the exercises had me lifting my legs in ways designed to show off my ass. The belt already made me conscious of it, and both the unnatural poses and the knowledge that I was being watched only made it more sexual.

We'd go from the warm-ups to practicing some of the routines I was going to use. Don was a big help in showing me the most effective ways to move around the stage while I spoke, even though there was no real choreography to be done.

Now, after the erotic warm-ups, I began to find myself standing and giving Don my safe-sex talk. I would look right at him, talking about all the sexual potential that still existed for gay men. I'd look down at his tightly curled hair, his brown eyes, his muscled arms, naked in his short-sleeved shirt, and the message started to become extremely personal.

I never got a hint from Don that he was responding, though. In fact, I never had been sure that he was actually gay. The close inspection he gave my body could merely have been professional interest. I had to consider the possibility, any way. There always had been many other people (of both sexes) around the practice room, and he seemed to treat them all in the same way. I simply could not get a reading on him.

Even his positive remarks about what I was going to be doing were pretty noncommittal. When it came down to it, there seemed to be only one thing that Don was interested in: work. The fact that work involved other people's bodies was simply coincidental.

Finally my last day of lessons arrived. I showed up, right on time. Don was waiting: everything as usual. Since my tour date was approaching, we'd agreed that I would go into more rehearsals later. Don would come by when I was in the final stages and be available if he thought I needed some more specific coaching.

I went through the regular warm-ups with him standing there in front of me. For some reason his body seemed closer this time than it had before. He moved to my side, and his own dance belt was clearly visible under the tights he was wearing. I was wondering . . . no . . . We'd been doing this for weeks, and he hadn't shown any indication that he was interested at all.

I moved to the barre and started the next round of movements. These were the ones that made me feel so awkward and . . . big. Usually my muscles were something I was proud of; after all, they were the result of a lot of effort. But working at the barre only made them seem like a lot of heavy baggage.

Don was right there with his stick. Usually he pointed or adjusted an arm with it. Today he seemed to have different ideas.

To my surprise I felt it move slowly up and down the curve of my ass. I kept on with my exercises not sure of what to do. The stick kept on moving as well.

"The wonderful thing about dance is the way it develops the buttock muscles. No other form of exercise ever seems to work so well."

So much for mystery.

I stopped what I was doing and turned to look at him. He still had that drill-instructor arrogance about him. But now there was the definite air of sexual interest in his stance as well.

What should I do? I wondered. Then I realized that my cock was answering for me. The charge in the atmosphere was no illusion. Neither was the strangling sensation my crotch was feeling as it was trapped in the tight dance belt.

I smiled—foolishly. There was just the bare hint of a break in his facade. "Your gluteal muscles seem to have benefited especially well in a short time."

I looked at him blankly.

"You've got a nice ass, Swann!" he said, laughing at the way my jaw had dropped.

Moving closer, he put one of his hands on my rear. He squeezed it appreciatively. "I think it might be a very interesting experiment to find out just how beneficial your movement exercises have been in terms of how you've learned to use this newly increased muscle mass."

This time I didn't wait for him to explain. "You want to fuck."

He smiled now. Moving closer, he kissed me. His skin was even smoother than I thought it'd be. He pulled away. "I thought you'd never catch on."

"Come on, Don," I said as I moved away. "I really mean all this safe-sex stuff I'm preaching. I'm not just playing around with it. You know that fucking's out."

"Look, you may not like taking a shower in a raincoat, but you still can take a shower."

I looked at him quizzically. I didn't have any idea what he was talking about.

"'Taking a shower in a raincoat' is a slang expression for wearing a rubber," he said, laughing. "There are such things as condoms, Glenn."

I mumbled out my confession: "I've never used one."

He stopped laughing to stare at me. "Are you one of those guys who are uptight about it?"

I admitted I felt weird about suddenly starting to use condoms at my age and with my supposedly great experience.

"No time like the present. Time for a final lesson in Don's dance class. Follow me."

I walked with him into his office. The walls were covered with posters advertising performances he'd appeared in at Lincoln Center and other places. It was a large room with a desk on one side and a couch and chairs on the other. I looked at the couch in an entirely new light.

Don went to his briefcase, putting it on his desk. "Never leave home without these, Glenn." He unsnapped the case and opened it, taking out a handful of wrapped squares and putting them on the desktop. "You certainly have to make that part of your lecture. So what do you know? Anything at all?"

"No. I just never had to learn."

"Well, nowadays you *do* have to learn. I'll give you the quick and easy introductory course." He picked one of the squares up. "There are two basic condoms you can buy. One is made of latex, the other of sheepskin. There are lots of variations on those themes, but the basic materials are almost always the same.

"Forget all the fancy ones. You don't need 'French ticklers' and all that stuff. You only need the basics. You can use the sheepskin if you want. Some people use them because they think they're more 'natural' and they claim they feel that way. But I'll warn you about one problem: If you want to start out with some oral sex, you'll hate them. The taste is the worst you could imagine.

"Untreated, unlubricated latex is just pure plastic. You can get it in your mouth, and if you just let your mind go, you can use it orally and get a great kick out of sucking cock, just like in the old days. Let me show you. Strip out of those tights and get out of that dance belt."

The dance master/drill sergeant was back in charge again. I followed orders as quickly as I had in boot camp. I pulled off the clothing I had and stood there, nude. "Nice raw material to work with." He smiled as he reached over and took hold of my cock. I was already getting excited by the closeness of our bodies and the anticipation of what would follow.

He let go of me just long enough to take off his own clothes. I eyed the closed door, worried. There were usually lots of other people around. "No problem," he said, reading my concern. "No one's due here for a while."

Soon he was naked and standing in front of me. He took his own cock in one hand, and mine in the other. He studied the two of them intently, obviously pleased to be giving his little lesson.

His cock was more responsive than mine. It arched up in its chocolate-colored fullness. I reached over and touched it. As always, I found the kinky pubic hair an exotic touch to a man's body. As soon as I'd made that sexual contact, my own erection filled out.

"Nice," he said softly. "Very nice." He took one of the wrapped condoms and opened it. He took the rolled up piece of latex in his hand and put it at the head of my erection. "You just start like this and unroll it," he said, demonstrating as he spoke.

"There's no big deal about it." He was right. The latex stretched over the head and then down the shaft as he unrolled. I had thought a condom would be as far from erotic as could be, but as I watched the white latex extend over my flesh, I began to feel differently. Instead of the humiliating "raincoat," I was seeing it as a kind of decoration.

Don must have been thinking along the same lines. He knelt down and took my now covered cock in his mouth. For a moment the contact felt strange, different from what I was used to, without the intense actual touch of his tongue and lips on my cock. But as soon as his body heat was conveyed through the latex to my skin, there was no lack of sensation. Not at all!

He kept up the sucking so long and with such expertise that my breathing started to increase in tempo. This was great! I'd had some guys go down on me lately—we'd mutually agreed that it was a decent risk as long as neither of us came in the other's mouth—but I hadn't been given a good, old-fashioned blow job in a long, long time. Even if the guys had liked it, there was that danger in the air that made us all less than spontaneous. But with the rubber Don obviously felt like he could go to town—and he sure did.

He stopped just in time. I was sure I was going to come any minute. He was smiling again and had to use his forearm to wipe away the saliva that was running down his mouth.

He reached for another rubber and this time put it on himself, explaining as he did it how it was rolled down over the shaft until it was stretched out to its furthest limit.

"See this small bit of plastic at the end?" he asked, holding the little nub that wasn't tightly stretched over his cock. "This is called the 'reservoir.' When you come, if this isn't here, the force of your ejaculation could break the condom, especially if you're one of the guys who shoots a big load of stuff. But this takes the pressure off.

"When you put on a rubber, you have to be very careful not to let any air get trapped inside the reservoir. It also could cause too much pressure, and there goes your protection. The best thing is to squeeze it tightly when you start unrolling the rubber. Then you won't have any problems."

There was little doubt what he had in mind now. Finished talking, he stood holding his hard cock in his hand.

I got down on my knees and took the anxious flesh in my mouth. My mouth slid over the plastic covering. There was no question that I missed the familiar and wonderful taste of a man's flesh; that was something that had always appealed to me. But there was still lots while I was going at it to remind me of the joys of getting it on orally with someone.

There was the wonderful smell of sex. Don's pubic hair was glistening with drops of sweat, and the funky smell of a man's crotch filled my nose as I moved up and down his shaft, my head bumping into his belly when I would get the whole length in my mouth. There was the sight of the low-hung testicles moving up and down with our joint motions.

After I was into it awhile I realized that my tongue could still make out the veins and the other distinguishing parts of the hard cock. I couldn't make believe that the rubber wasn't there, but so was his cock, just for me.

I could feel Don's hands reach down under my arms and lift me up. I hated letting it go, but he had other ideas. When I was standing, we kissed. Don started edging me toward that suspicious couch. I can't say I was resisting.

He moved me so that I was facedown on the cushions. I'd rather have been on the other side of this one, but he *was* the teacher, I reminded myself. I felt as much as heard him move back to his case and get out some lubricant. My cock was hard. The position he'd put me in left one of my knees on the floor, the other leg stretched down the length of the sofa. The result was that my ass was totally open. I could actually feel a small breeze moving around the hairs that surrounded my sphincter.

When he came back, he reached down and rubbed some cool grease onto my hole. He moved over me, his knees inside my thighs. I could feel the tip of him as he began to press it against the protecting muscles. Then there was the expected sharp sensation of something entering my body. It had become very unfamiliar in the past few years.

I moaned at the intrusion. Then there was only the sensation of being filled up as he slid farther and farther into me. I could feel his hand; he was gripping the base of his cock. I knew he was doing that to hold the condom in place. It was one of the important things about using rubbers. They were no good if you let them slip too much.

Lessons in how to use rubbers were pretty far from my mind, though. I had to admit that all I could concentrate on was the feel of Don in me, on me, around me.

His curly body hair rubbed against my back and my ass. He was moving with slow, gentle motions, making love, not just fucking hard and furious.

The feeling of getting fucked was overwhelming me. I lifted up my midsection to greet the welcome thrusts. He was kissing my shoulders and the back of my neck as he moved, making sure that all of me was being paid attention to.

Then came that quickening of his breath. I could feel a surge run through his body as his muscles tensed. He let out a quick, harsh yell, and finally his body collapsed on top of mine.

After a couple of calm and wonderful minutes—those times when fucking is best, with a slackening cock inside you—he began to pull out. When he passed that last grip of the sphincter, we both sighed with a little relief—and a little sadness that it was finished.

Well, at least one part was finished.

Don slowly moved me over onto my back. My cock was still covered with its own condom, and it was still rock-hard. He played with it a bit. I thought he might just masturbate me. Not that I was about to argue. Any relief would be welcome.

Instead he picked up the lubricant and took out some to smear on my latex-covered erection. Then he lifted himself up with that grace of a well-trained dancer. Kneeling over my erection, he held it straight up in the air. Staring intently into my eyes, he used all of his body's skills to lower himself onto me.

Now it was my turn to feel that initial resistance of tight muscles. It was my turn to feel the sudden heat of a man's insides as they encased my cock.

"Hold it firmly," he said. I knew he meant for me to grab the bottom of the condom and keep it in place. As soon as I did, I got to see the most powerful dance performance of my life.

He was right about the way that dance can develop ass muscles. It wasn't just a question of making them look good; believe me, they can start doing tricks. I had never been with a man who was able to increase and decrease the pressure of fucking with his buttock muscles the way that Don did that morning.

He would rise up and then lower himself again and again. He'd hold my erection so tight that it was close to the point of pain, then release it so that all it could feel was the sensation of his body heat.

I wanted it to go on and on, but I couldn't. I just couldn't withstand the intense sexuality of his agile contortions. I came, lifting up my hips (and him with them) when the surge of my orgasm went through my body.

Afterward we got dressed slowly. "Not a bad pupil," he said.

"It's all in the teaching," I teased back.

"Glenn, there's one more thing I should tell you about. The lubricant I used isn't just anything off the shelf. It's got something called nonoxyodol-9. It's a spermicide. It's an extra ounce of protection. Use it. The proof's not all in, and since it is a detergent chemical, it might irritate your insides. But if it doesn't bother you, it can help a lot. You can get it at any drugstore."

"You're a constant font of information."

"Well, I certainly felt like a fountain today. And if you got some decent information out of it—great. I got something more than a little decent info myself."

CHAPTER SEVEN

TIME TO PUT ON THE SHOW

I was finally ready to start touring. All the groundwork had been done; I had gotten all the chances for training and rehearsal I was going to have.

The first round of appearances were at the Club Body Center in Miami. The owner, Jack Campbell, had financed the creation of Mr. Safe Sex and wanted to use my personna as a means to educate his customers. This was just the beginning, I could tell. The very idea of having someone act like the Smokey the Bear of safe sex had captured a lot of people's imaginations, it seemed. I was glad that I was going to have a chance to talk to so many people.

Still, all those fine sentiments didn't help my nervousness at all. The first night in Miami, I stood backstage, drenched in sweat and stage fright. Great for the image, I thought to myself. Mr. Safe Sex is too anxious to walk out and talk to you—let alone give demonstrations.

But I knew this was one date I had to keep. I could be as apprehensive as I wanted to, but my assignation was with an entire audience, not just one person. I had to show up.

I listened to the introductions being made. They were my cue that I was going to have to get out there soon. I had decided to use my old rank in the Marine Corps as part of my stage act: I was not just Mr. Safe Sex, I was also Sergeant Glenn Swann. I pulled on my Marine jacket—basically all I was wearing, besides the jock—and stood looking at myself in the mirror.

When they put me through Camp Lejeune, I thought this was not quite the image they'd been expecting to get. But I had to admit that it was a fine reflection of the best of the Marine tradition, all the same. I was going out there, and I was going to be giving the most important pep talk I could to the guys who were going to have to fight a very difficult war. I was going to arm them with my own special ammunition— information and education. We were going to stick to one another as if we were a unit that needed to act as an integrated whole. We were in this thing together.

Thinking about it that way did me a world of good. I winked at myself in the mirror, just as they were making the last announcement. It was time to go out and face the music.

As I walked onto the stage there was a round of applause. I was prepared for the racy remarks that were instantly hurled at me. Plenty of people would put down anything that happened in a place like this. But as I stood there I realized that I was on one of the most important stages I could be on.

True, plenty of places had safe-sex material and other AIDS information available for the asking. But the guys who were in this audience weren't necessarily the ones who would read or hear that information. They were a different group from most gay men and my entire Mr. Safe Sex persona had been designed especially to reach them.

I ignored the remarks, letting them fly through the air. Deliberately I chose the harsh exterior I'd learned from the drill instructors in the Corps. Their example had shown me that you could win over a lot of people simply by your presentation. If you take yourself seriously, no matter what the context, the people eventually will have to understand that they're going to have to take you seriously too.

The crowd died down a little bit as their reactions to my hard image began to sink in. I was *feeling* like a DI. I knew they were waiting for me to strip down even more than I was already: They were just expecting another porn show. Well, they were going to get more than they had bargained for.

I stood up to my full height, pulling in my stomach and throwing out my chest. I bellowed at them in the best Lejeune tradition: *"You can't do those things anymore!"*

If there had been any doubt in their minds about my being earnest about this presentation, that moment erased it. "We have buddies who are in trouble and we have to help them!" I went on. "We have to learn how to take care of ourselves, and we have to learn how to be careful of others as well!"

I began to move around the stage. I was feeling the role now. I couldn't see them too well on the other side of the bright lights, but I could feel every one of them looking right at me. I didn't want to blow this chance to get my message across.

"Stop doing the things that make you and our buddies sick! No more fucking without rubbers! No more taking loads of cum down your throat or up your ass! No more rimming! Those things are *over!*

"Do you understand?"

There was nothing but shocked silence on the other side of the lights. I wondered if I'd gone too far. But I was on a roll and I wasn't going to stop now.

"I can't hear you. *Do you understand?"*

Just like boot camp, there were a few guys in the audience

who murmured some affirmation. But most were still too stunned at the idea that I was talking to them this way in a place that used to be a bathhouse.

"I still can't hear you. *Do you understand?*"

Now there was a real response. A mixed chorus of "Yes, sir" and "Okay, okay" came from the group.

"That's better," I announced. I was walking around the stage with my cockiest walk now. I had their attention after that. Of course, there were other elements that helped make sure that they were concentrating on what I had to say. My outfit didn't hurt.

I had on my Marine jacket, my military boots, and not a hell of a lot more. In fact, the only other thing was a jockstrap. I guess I'm putting it mildly when I say that they were studying me closely.

I stalked the stage once again, getting more and more into it all. Then I went to the tall stool that was in the center. The room was so quiet, I could hear the wood creak when I sat down.

All the lessons I'd learned were flashing through me. Also, I was surprised to find myself getting off on the idea of all these men watching me. I liked the exhibitionism of it all, the fact that my body and my sexuality could attract them. I felt myself getting hard in the jock, which made me feel even more confident.

I stared past the lights and broke into a smile. "But, fellas, let me tell you what you still *can* do."

They broke out into a cheer as I opened up my Marine jacket and showed my bare chest. I ran my hand over my stomach and up to my nipples, remembering the sensations that Mike had created when he'd first shown me what potential they had.

But the crowd really went wild when my hand moved back down and disappeared into my jock. That was what they were waiting for, and Mr. Safe Sex had no intention of leaving them unsatisfied. None at all.

Some friends had a party for me after my "debut" on stage. Zack and Don teased me about how much my new persona was going to enhance my own sex life. They didn't realize how much I already understood about that. I'd already had plenty of evidence that being open made others feel less self-conscious about their own sexual desires. But the teasing made me remember some other things as well— things that weren't always as pleasant.

When I'd first started posing in erotic magazines and appeared in my first movie, there had been a lot of very hot men who'd been interested in me. I liked the attention and loved the idea that I was one of the desired men after the exposure I'd gotten—and was given.

But there was a price to be paid. There were a lot of men who only wanted to get to know me because I was an image of a certain kind. They wanted to be able to have sex with the man they fantasized about in the gay magazines. Often it was a kind of trophy hunt for them.

With some men—certainly ones like Zack and Mike—an honest exchange of sexual pleasure between buddies was something that I valued. It didn't have to get all involved in love, romance, and the rest of those emotions. But when others weren't honest, then all kinds of problems arose, which usually involved being hurt and feeling downright lousy.

I'd had my fill of those situations and had learned to avoid them. But there was also Mike's comment about the theatrics of sex. I had been intrigued by that. I knew that there were benefits to playing out our own personal psychodramas. It seemed to me that I should be attuned to those people who'd be interested in it. I was also curious how it would work and what it would feel like.

Those ideas were floating through my mind at the party as I kept moving around, being introduced to new people. I met some guys I'd expect to find there, the types who wanted nothing but the appeal of star-fucking and who made that desire obvious. I'd had a hard time with that type before, now it was a type I wasn't interested in at all anymore.

There were also a lot of men who just liked having a good time talking to anyone who'd been up on a stage. Full of jokes and teasing remarks that I knew were meant well, they were easy to take.

I was also used to the leering comments that anyone who's taken his clothes off on stage or in front of a camera gets. There were always plenty of people who thought if you did *that*, you were available for the asking. Actually, it was those guys who bothered me the most. I didn't like the idea of anyone assuming that my body wasn't something I had control over. Getting into performances—I don't care what kind they are—doesn't mean that you've given up the right to privacy when you leave the arena where your act took place. As usual, I moved away from those guys fast.

By the time the party was really going full blast, I had ended up standing in a corner. The men had gotten over the novelty of being introduced to me, and they had moved on to the next stage of their evenings—either talking to their old friends or getting to know new ones.

After the flurry of activity I'd started off with, I was happy to have a bit of a rest from it all. I felt like I was melting back into a crowd. I was dressed simply, just slacks and a sports shirt. Mr. Safe Sex was receding from his stage, and his public was giving him a break. Or at least most of it was.

I became aware of one guy standing near me who obviously didn't want me to drift away. He was younger than I

was. I didn't pay much attention at first. I was vaguely aware
of his eyes on me, though, as more time went on, I realized
that he wasn't interested in anything or anyone but me.

Eventually he moved closer, finally getting around to in-
troducing himself. His name was Sam, he said, and he was a
student at one of the nearby colleges. At first I just chatted
with him. He was very good looking in a preppy, clean-cut
way, but he was younger than my usual type. I guessed he
was about twenty-one. No matter what his age might be, he
was pretty insistent in his cruising. I wondered if he was just
interested in me because of my momentary celebrity.

When the conversation came around to safe sex, he was
the one who brought it up—he may have been using it only
as a come-on, but if so, he was pretty good with his tech-
nique. Still, there was something about his heightened manner of speaking that made me think that more was going on
than I was seeing. He was standing very close to me, so
close that at times we were almost touching, though our
communication was only verbal—so far.

"This whole safe-sex thing is just as hard for those of us
who've just come out," he was saying to me. "You guys keep
on talking about the things that you've had to give up, but
we've never even experienced them. They're like some kind
of mythology from an ancient time.

"When I listened to your speech about 'what used to go
on,' Glenn, it was all foreign to me. There aren't dens of
anonymous sex that any sane person would go into anymore.
The days of all that faceless cruising you talk about are
something we don't even understand. Coming out in the
middle of all this is a bummer, and that's putting it mildly."

I wasn't at all sure I liked the sudden role of older man
that he was giving me. I also was not sure if I liked how very
close in front of me he was standing. He was blond and
blue-eyed. His beard was slight, so close-shaven that his

facial skin appeared totally smooth. I could see through his polo shirt that he was firmly built. The loose cotton hung vaguely on the well-developed chest. He'd said he was on the swin team in school, with the pectorals he was showing, the trim waist and firm legs, I could well believe it.

"Well, I know the benefits aren't exciting to a lot of guys," I said weakly, trying to defend the situation. "But we are drawing closer as a community. We are helping each other— we're learning to take a lot more emotional and sexual care of one another than we used to do."

He shrugged, not at all convinced by what I'd said. But he wasn't so angry about life that he was giving up on his options. He still had a gleam in his eye. I realized that he was testing me. I wondered what the test was really about.

"One of the things that I regret missing is the possibility of all that *play* that went on," he said. "When people were in those arenas where they didn't have to know one another and where the rules about sex and behavior were relaxed, they could get into their fantasies more and let themselves go. That's harder now.

"There are so few times when there's still the idea of the play. Your show was part of it."

There! He was finally going to get to the point. "How so?" I wanted to prime him some more.

"The uniform and the way you present yourself as the big, tough Marine. I bet you did that in the back rooms in the days when they were hot and popular. I got off on that. I got off on that a lot."

His intent stare was conveying how much this meant to him. I stared back at him. This might just be the kind of theatrics that Larry had meant.

"Oh, yeah," I said, letting my voice drop to an even lower octave than usual. "How?"

His eyes lit up at the hint that I might just go along with

him. "I knew you'd been through boot camp—you had to
have been, you had the uniform on. The idea of someone
like that taking over some young recruit, putting him through
the paces—that's hot, man. I get off on that. Just the idea of
the uniform is something I get off on, if you want to know
the truth. The rest is icing on the cake."

"Because of the way you can imagine yourself really performing it?"

"Yeah." I knew he was affecting a punk attitude, as deliberately as I now purposely lowered my voice to him. He was
throwing down a gauntlet and daring me to pick it up.

This could be fun.

"You know, now that I'm leaving Miami for my tour,
there's not going to be anyone around here to do the work
that has to be done. I was thinking about finding someone
else who could be the local Mr. Safe Sex, someone who had
the knowledge and the ability to project a healthy attitude to
the public."

"Oh?" He kept the air of challenge in his voice.

"Yeah. But he'd have to be someone who could really do
it. I'd have to trust him to carry off the act seriously and to
be a decent representative of all we're standing for. He'd
probably have to go through a pretty grueling training period on top of everything else. And he'd certainly have to go
through an evaluation."

"You make it sound like going into the service."

"Well, in its own way it is like that. You know—marshaling
our forces and defining our strategy, doing our recruiting
and making sure the troops have the proper training. All of
that translates when we start talking about the educational
work that has to be done."

I was sure there was no doubt in his mind about what I
was up to; he was right there with me. "Think I might have a
chance to do it? I wouldn't mind trying out for the part."

"I don't know. You young guys haven't always exactly stood up for a guy in uniform." I was surprised to note that he actually looked hurt when I said that. "But I suppose we could see if you understood what might be involved in a bit of a military life fighting for safe sex."

"When's the physical?" He was smirking now but not so broadly that he seemed to be taking the game lightly. After all, he had been the one to set it up.

"No time like the present. This party's going to break up soon enough, anyway."

"You're on, Sergeant Swann. You got one recruit reporting for duty."

Theatre, I kept on reminding myself as we went back to my own nearby apartment. *Stay in the role. Make this an extension of your act.*

I understood how powerful fantasies could be for many gay men. That was part of the reason I was encouraging this guy. It was like my own training for doing the stage act. You had to learn how to feel comfortable, and you had to trust the other person to get into it with you. Sam had given me plenty of indication about his own fantasies. What he was doing was inviting me to go along for the ride with him. If I wanted to, I could enter into his erotic world with him; at least I could be a buddy and get him off by supporting his own imaginative sexual creations.

The uniform was a big part of it; that was clear. I had my Marine jacket slung over my shoulder as we walked to my place. As soon as I'd unlocked the door and we'd gotten inside, I took off my shirt and slipped the jacket off. He came to me, knowing now just how much I was going to play into his fantasy games, and his arms went around my waist. His head rested on my chest. I knew that what he was doing was partly his desire to touch the uniform and partly his appetite for physical affection.

I let him have his way for a short while. Not for too long, though—I had been playing back the rest of what he'd said as well, and he was going to be recruit-for-a-night, just the way he wanted.

"Get to the middle of the room and shuck those clothes, boy." I talked to him with that same deep rattle that my own drill instructor had used on us. His body went stiff with a sudden combination of shock and thrill at my words.

He pulled back from me and stood still for just a moment. Then he moved quickly to the center of the living area. While he quickly pulled his shirt up off his body, I set the rheostats on my overhead lighting so that he was standing in a close enough approximation of a spotlight to feed our inventiveness.

By the time I was finished with my task, so was he. He was doing his civilian's best to assume attention. His shoulders were squared and pulled back, his firm stomach muscles were contracted inward as much as he could, and his arms were straight against his sides. He was looking forward in an exaggerated manner. His chin was even pushed down against his neck. This was his image of a military posture—and it wasn't too far off.

I walked over to him and slowly circled around his naked body. It was handsome, smooth-skinned, and constructed of those firm but spongy muscles that swimmers have. The best part of a swimmer's physique is its visual impact. He had the expansive chest, I saw. But he also had the sleek and molded leg muscles, the high and rounded ass that a combination of years of swimming and youth had created so perfectly.

I stifled a smile when I realized that another part of him was approaching attention as well. He didn't have an enormous cock, but the one he had was beautifully proportioned. Cleanly circumcised, it was arching out away from his body as his excitement became more and more obvious.

"You think your mommy's going to pick up for you, boy?" I said. "What are your clothes doing messing up my floor?"

He scurried to pick them up and take them to the nearest piece of furniture. "Fold them," I ordered, just the way I had been warned in the service.

He went about his task quickly and efficiently. Then he moved back to the middle of my makeshift spotlight and resumed his former posture. "Not bad," I murmured. I wondered if he was getting the same pleasure from a be-grudging compliment that I remembered having the first time I'd been given a kind word in the service.

"Now, why are you volunteering for this safe-sex service?" I demanded, still using my best DI's voice.

"Well, sir, I want to do my part." He stumbled through the words. "I want to be part of the team."

"You think you understand the rules?"

"Yes, sir. I've studied them and made them a part of my life since I came out."

"We'll see about that later. Right now I want to examine the raw materials. Spread your legs; hands behind your neck. *Now!*"

His youthful body sprang into action as he jumped to comply. He moved so quickly that his tight balls and half-hard cock were still bouncing when he was in the position I had told him I wanted. I moved up until I was right in front of him.

I ran a hand over his chest. There were only a few strands of blond hair on it, swirled around his flat, round, dark nipples. My hand moved with military authority; this wasn't the time for the gentle explorations of romance. I slid my hand over his stomach and to his sides. I bent over slightly so I could feel the back of his legs. They were especially well-developed from his swimming.

I moved around to the back of him. His shoulders were a

fan of wide muscle that dove into his waist and then, once there, rounded out over a beautiful ass made more noticeable by the sharp tan line of his racing brief. Everywhere the brief had not covered his skin was a deep brown. But where it had protected him, the flesh glowed white, looking almost bright in the overhead light.

I reached up and put my arms around him. My hands found the twin curves of his chest, and I placed my palms over the smooth nipples. I pinched them slightly, just enough to get a good sigh out of him. I released my hold then and walked back around to face him.

"So you like the uniform?"

"Yes, sir."

"And you think you want to sign up for this safe-sex position?"

"Yes, sir."

I didn't have to hear the words. His cock was hard and erect, standing straight out from his belly now. There was even a small drop of clear precum seeping from the head, as the final proof of Sam's sincere appreciation for what we were doing.

I reached over and took a hold of his erection. The feel was even silkier than most. The skin was so starkly pale that the veins that roped around the shaft were clearly visible blue lines.

"Sir?" he said through clenched teeth.

"Yes?"

"I think, sir, that we're going to have a problem if you keep on holding me that way."

I smiled at him and let go. He let out a sharp breath of relief. "Seems to me we have to have some lessons in self-control here."

"Well, sir, I think the control would be okay if you weren't the one doing the holding." He couldn't help but break out of the scene and smile at that one.

I was getting pretty hot by now. The sexual air was thick. I was happy to give Sam his military fantasy, and it was really working; but I didn't think we needed to go any further into it. There were more pressing issues that were coming to the fore now—like my own erection.

I stepped out of my loafers and dropped my slacks. Pulling down my briefs, I stood before him, wearing only my jacket. I crossed my arms over my chest. "Why don't you try out something more real now?"

He looked at me, not quite sure what I meant but obviously interested in the hard evidence of my own excitement. "Come on over and let's work those two hard cocks," I finally said.

He relaxed from his position and moved toward me. His hands unbuttoned my jacket and pulled it apart. He leaned over enough to suck in one of my nipples. His teeth played with it gently. The sharp edges pulled me into a surge of erotic response.

His other hand had moved down and grabbed hold of my cock. He was gently pulling and pushing it with a firm grip on the shaft. The head would occasionally graze against the wisps of hair on his abdomen.

He moved back, letting my erect nipple free. I looked down at him. My face was intent but not from military games anymore. It was excitement, pure and simple, that was controlling me now.

I reached down and let my lips run across his. He moved his hands, and I felt his own hard cock pressed against mine, both of them in his tight grip. He was manipulating them back and forth at the same time.

The sensation of our two erections touching so completely and sharing the same stimulation was an intimacy unlike any other I'd felt. I reached down and took hold of his balls. The two ovals were held tightly in his young skin, soft underneath a slight patch of pubic hair. I got hold of my own and stretched our sacs slightly so we could feel our testicles touching, just as our cocks were.

I listened as the pace of his breathing increased. He was getting as close to coming as I was. I moved my head back to touch his lips with mine once more. It was just in time. I felt the hot flow of his seminal fluid spurt onto me. He moved more quickly now as my grip on our balls tightened. He was able to use his cum as a lubricant. The fluid let his hands slither over the length of my cock. In just a minute I was shooting my own pleasure over him. It brought out a deep sound of passion, as intense as the moans that had announced his own orgasm.

"Have a good time, recruit?"

Sam smiled as we stood in the doorway. He had dressed after his shower, to get home to his own apartment in order to be ready for an early class the next day. "The best, Sarge. And, look, if you meant it about taking over some of your Mr. Safe Sex stuff here in town while you're away, I'm really interested."

"I'll have to talk to Jack Campbell and the others at the Club Body Center, but I think it's a good idea. Who knows? Maybe I will enlist an army for this. I could leave little detachments of Mr. Safe Sex volunteers around the country."

"Just remember where the founding branch is, Sarge. And make sure you come back for an inspection pretty soon. After all, you never know when the troops might need a refresher course."

CHAPTER EIGHT

PUTTING A TEAM TOGETHER

My first tour took me from Houston and New Orleans up the Mississippi Valley into the Midwest. At each stop I'd perform, putting on my act and giving my lectures on the new forms of sexuality that gay men were going to have to embrace.

I became more comfortable with the performances. At the same time, though, I had trouble with the growing notoriety I was receiving. Sometimes it seemed that being publicly identified as Mr. Safe Sex was harder than actually getting up on a stage in a closed room. I'd be pointed out in restaurants and winked at on the street. When the greetings were coming from gay guys whom I knew were being supportive, I enjoyed it. Yet I was also doing television and newspaper interviews, and many of the people looking at me so closely weren't at all sympathetic to what I was trying to do. And they showed it.

But the work went on. So did the fun and the unexpected events that came with all the work.

The idea of recruiting a local Mr. Safe Sex was agreed to

enthusiastically by the promoters. From now on, we decided, I would make soliciting the volunteers part of my show. A lot of people gave me grief about it, like Zack.

"Hell, Glenn, you're attracting enough of the action as it is with your fame," he complained. "Leave something for the rest of us."

Actually, one of my first experiences lining up recruits for the movement was more than I had bargained for.

I certainly had known that I wasn't the only person involved in encouraging various educational safe-sex programs— far from it. There were many men like me all around the country. I read the publications that were coming out and met a number of the people who were giving lectures and workshops on the topic.

There had also been stories in the various gay newspapers about some groups that were involved in putting together safe-sex parties. That idea had appealed to me but I'd thought that those parties were happening only in New York, Los Angeles, and San Francisco.

I was wrong. During one of the first stops on my tour a man came up to me after my presentation. Smiling, with a playful seduction in his voice, he said he'd like to talk to me about the idea of taking on my role in that city. I told him I'd talk as soon as I could get cleaned up and changed.

I came out and met him in the coffee shop. He was sitting at a table with about a half dozen other men. I went up to them and was introduced around. The guy who'd made the initial approach was named Terry.

"I have to admit that there's a catch to the idea of being the local Mr. Safe Sex," Terry said. He was about thirty and was wearing the costume of the urban gay man: tank top, tight button-fly jeans, boots. He had a good tan and a nice body, the kind that seemed to come from work, not the sculpted form that a gym produces.

I didn't understand what he was getting at. He hastened to clarify his dilemma. "Well," he explained, "all of us here would like to have the job; collectively, I guess.

"You see, we'd begun all this safe-sex stuff over a year ago. We have a little club that has weekly meetings. It's a get-together for those of us who didn't want to give up the excitement of group sex but who knew that we had to change the ground rules for it if we wanted to stay healthy."

This was getting interesting. It got even more intriguing when Terry told me that they were having a meeting that very night. They'd pushed back their usual starting hour so they could see my show—"And try to get you to come along with us afterward," Terry admitted.

They were obviously committed to the safe-sex guidelines I was promoting. The idea that they had moved it into a party atmosphere was something that I wanted to know more about.

I agreed to join them, and we all left in a group for Terry's house, their usual meeting place. "I've done over my base-ment for the Club," he said as we drove through the city streets. "I consider it my contribution to the cause." He was partly kidding, but he meant it as well.

His middle-class house was in an almost suburban neigh-borhood. There were already some people waiting. Terry explained that his lover had gone straight home to get things ready as well as to be there when the members arrived. The crowd was sitting around the living room. Some were drink-ing beer; others had soft drinks in their hands. The spirit was decidedly up, and the atmosphere was pure party.

I took a cola and went around to be introduced to some of the more than twenty-five men who were in the room. "Some others are already downstairs, getting ready," Terry told me.

I was given a sheet with the rules of the Club on it. They

were even more strict than some other guidelines I'd seen: No oral contact below the waist at all. No deep kissing. No fucking at all, rubbers or not. It wasn't just a series of safe-sex guidelines, I realized. It was as much a setting of the parameters that would encourage everyone to take part in a group activity. I wasn't going to have any trouble with any of it.

I looked around and saw that the men were at least as appealing a group as any I'd seen assembled in a bar. I especially liked the combination of light sexual anticipation and friendship that characterized how they interacted with one another. There were hands resting on legs more intimately than you'd see in a regular party, and more than a few playful gropes as well.

I could sense myself getting ready for the action to start. There was a cheer when Terry made the announcement that they were ready. A bunch of guys started to move to the stairway. One I had been talking to took me by the arm and led me toward the line that already had formed.

When we got to the bottom of the stairs, there was a poster with an arrow pointing to a coatroom where everyone was ordered to leave their clothing. I thought the undressing was a little sudden and was somewhat disappointed when I realized that I wasn't going to get to see a careful, erotic group strip. Instead it was more like walking into a locker room. It had its attractions, don't misunderstand, but it wasn't what I'd been envisioning.

The rules did say that you could leave on a few pieces of clothing if they were a part of some sort of sexual outfit. Now I understood why some of the guys had brought small bags with them. Inside were their fantasy clothes. I hadn't even known about that part of the activity. I simply stripped in front of some attentive eyes and walked, naked, into the play area.

I got a fresh cola from the bar and took a seat. The heat was turned way up. Obviously this had been done to make the nude men more physically comfortable. It had the added effect of producing a good, strong male scent right from the start.

I sat there, seeing before me an incredible array of costumed men. If I had thought the mood was too casual before, I now understood that I had underestimated some of Larry's drama lessons.

He'd explained to me that when people move onto a stage, they cross an imaginary line. That line was the demarcation of their character. The little drama that Sam and I had enacted followed the same principles. I'd put my military coat back on, I'd set the stage for him and his imagination.

These men were doing that for one another with pieces of clothing. There were some who wore only the smallest hint of raw material. I saw one guy walk in wearing nothing but a hard hat. I had thought that his two-day growth of beard was just an attempt to be stylish; it was the way that a lot of models were appearing in the magazines just then. But I suddenly suspected that it was something that he'd let grow just for tonight. With the rough beard and the construction worker's hat, suddenly he was a lot more masculine in a way than he had been when I'd seen him upstairs with his clothes on.

Two other men walked in wearing no more than pieces of leather. Obviously they were into a lot more of a scene than I was. The first guy had on a biker's hat and reflector glasses. He was wearing heavy motorcycle boots. His companion walked behind him, being led by a leash that was attached to a collar around his neck.

If the leather was more a fantasy made for someone other than me, the pair of guys who came in with cowboy hats and handkerchiefs around their necks were definitely my style.

Not that I minded the young guy who came in wearing a T-shirt and white socks that stretched up over his calves, either. For me, he certainly had the makings of a college jock—and all that went with it.

As they continued to come out of the dressing room and into the play area, the different men were turning into a cast of a fantasy movie. They were much more quiet now than they had been upstairs. After all, we were here for some serious sex, and we all knew it. It wasn't the time or place for any chitchat.

I wondered if there was going to be some kind of announcement made about starting. It became clear pretty quickly that the guys were used to just getting things going when they felt like it. Terry felt like it at that very moment.

He sat down beside me, as naked as I was. At just the same time another man took a seat on the other side. "Meet my lover, Luis."

Luis was about my age. His Latin heritage was evident in his soft brown skin, dark eyes, and dark hair. His sensual body was moving to the beat of the music on the stereo.

"Comfortable?" Luis asked me.

"Getting used to it," I answered. I was only *just* doing that. I enjoyed the sight of all the men crowding into the basement, but I was always on edge in group activities. Even when it had been more popular a few years ago, I hadn't ever really gotten into the idea of group sex.

Unlike me, Terry and Luis were anything but inhibited. Luis had put a heavy, warm arm over my shoulders. Terry had moved so his body was flush against mine, and one of his hands was snaking around my waist. He wasn't being coy about his goal; he rested the hand right on my thigh, only inches from my cock.

This time my cock was as unresponsive as it ever gets. True, it didn't actually shrink, but it did seem to want to disappear into my foreskin to hide from all these strangers. I fought back an urge to pat its head to let it know it didn't have to worry about what would happen to it.

There wasn't any lack of visual stimulation to go along with the physical activity coming at me from both sides; that wasn't the problem. The scene that the "master" and his "slave" were putting on in the far corner certainly had its appeal, even for someone who wasn't into leather. The master was standing behind the other guy, whose hands had been tied to a rafter above his head and had rawhide laces weaved around his cock and balls. He had put on heavy leather gloves and was roughly rubbing them over the bound captive's vulnerable body.

"That something you're into?" Terry whispered into my ear. He had seen me studying the action.

"No, not at all," I said.

"Don't worry, we let everyone go at their own pace. There are a lot of guys who like that kind of thing, and the rest of us—even if we don't want to partake—have to admit that it's hot to watch them."

I nodded. My once shy cock was beginning to stir back to life from viewing the two leather men going at one another.

They weren't the only ones who were putting on a show. The younger guy who I'd seen come in with the long socks and T-shirt was standing in front of a man who was obviously the complement to his own fantasy. This man was naked except for his shirt and dark glasses. A coach's whistle hung from his neck. He had placed his hands squarely on the sides of his body, assuming an arrogant posture toward the kid, who appeared to be acting with that same insolent attitude Sam had shown me.

This coach was even more adamant than I'd been in my drill-instructor role. In a flash he'd taken the guy by the waist and, having put his foot up on a chair, had thrown him over his knee. The room was full of the echoes of a good, hard spanking.

My cock was betraying even more interest in the action. "Are you sure you're not into these things?" Luis asked.

"Only to watch."

Luis just smiled. "You can watch all you want to, Glenn. Let me do all the work." His hand moved down and took a hold of my half-hard cock and my balls. He let my testicles slip from his grip and let his fingers wrap themselves around my penis. I waited for him to start jerking me off, but he didn't. He was content for the moment with just having that calm clasp on me.

I could feel myself responding to the human touch and knew I was getting harder. Terry was paying close attention to what was happening now. His arm tightened around my shoulders, and he drew me closer to him. Our lips met. My own arms gathered around him, and soon we were entwined with one another.

That was some kind of signal to Luis. As soon as he saw that his lover and I were embracing, he began to move his fist up and down my growing cock. He moved off the couch and knelt in front of me. His hand never stopped its movements, but now his mouth moved to one of my nipples. The feelings of my body being in intimate contact with both men were electric. But I hadn't realized yet that this was just the beginning.

The action our trio was getting into was a new signal to the rest of the group. The first scenarios we had all been watching had only begun to set the stage. Now it was time for everyone to get into the night's events.

I was so caught up in Luis and Terry that I was only vaguely aware of the other gathering bodies. But soon I felt another hand on my neck. Suddenly a second mouth started sucking on my other nipple.

All at once a sea of flesh seemed to be flowing around me. I could see bushes of pubic hair, images of well-defined biceps, the round, moonlike masses of buttocks as they began to move in from all directions.

Accompanying this was an assortment of other elements assaulting my senses. There was that strong male odor that the room's heat helped produce and, off in the distance, the added sound effects of flesh hitting flesh as the master and slave and the coach and athlete continued to play.

Somehow we slid off the couch and onto the floor. I was on my back, my arms still around Terry. There were still two unseen mouths at work on my nipples. I could feel a hand masturbating my cock while one was holding my balls and at least one more was feeling my buttocks. The sheer anarchy of the action was exhilarating. All around me I could hear the increasing tempo of the crowd's breathing.

Terry moved his face away from mine and knelt back on his haunches. His own cock was hugely erect, and he was jerking it with quick anxious motions. I could tell by the expression on his face that he was getting ready to come. As if he realized that his lover was getting close, Luis pulled back from my chest. I barely had time to think about it when someone else dived down to take his place.

The two men were on either side of me now. They were looking at me—studying my body and my own excitement with appreciative glances—and then eyeing each other. There was no denying the communication that was going on. Part of it was pure lust at the sight of each other's bodies, but there was also the kind of knowledge that only lovers could understand, the appreciation of what was going on through each other's minds.

They were getting closer and closer. So was I. I couldn't help but flash on the image of the leather action in the corner as someone's hand kept urging me to my orgasm. In a way I was helpless. I wasn't the one determining how fast or how hard the pressure was. Also, the sight of Terry and Luis mesmerized me. Being there was like my own form of S&M, waiting for them to come while at the same time my own cock was out of my power.

There was something especially hot about how close they were to me. I could see every detail of their cocks and balls while they continued their ferocious jerking off. Terry's dick was uncircumcised. The long foreskin easily moved up and down over the knob of his cock. Luis was uncut too. I wasn't used to that; most of the men I'd known had been circumcised. It made them seem all the more exotic.

The smell was getting stronger as the hand that gripped me made me more aware of my lack of control. I felt myself getting closer and closer to the edge.

Terry got there first. Closing his eyes, he threw back his head. In seconds there was a series of white, fluid waves pulsing out of him, right on to my chest.

The hot fluid hadn't even had a chance to cool before Luis let out a small animal yell and his own cum flowed onto me. The two loads of cum were too much. I felt my muscles contracting and tightening in that hard grip of orgasm, and then my own cum joined theirs on my stomach.

"Having a good time, Glenn?" Luis asked me later when we were upstairs. I'd left the continuing action in the basement, cleaned up, and gotten dressed.

"It's a trip," I had to admit. It has been quite an experience. In the old days there were bars and clubs all over the country where that kind of group scene had been the most sought-after sexual activity for gay men. Now this safe-sex group had brought it all back to mind in living color.

"Lots of the guys are hoping you're going to go on back down. They'd like to get to know you." Luis's sparkling eyes let me know precisely how those men wanted the relationships to progress.

"I'm afraid I've had it for tonight," I answered. It was the *truth*.

"A lot of people are going to be disappointed," Luis said. "They think you're supposed to be Mr. Safe Stud, not just Mr. Safe Sex."

"I have to be up early for some interviews in the morning and I'm really done in. I think it's time for me to get back to the hotel."

"Fine. Let me get a couple more things to cover my body and I'll give you a lift."

When we were in the car, Luis and I talked about Terry's suggestion that the group become more public about safe sex and even make some appearances. "It's fine with me," I said. "You guys certainly know what you're doing."

"Yeah. You know, I love it all. I really do. I look forward to these get-togethers we have every week. But to me it's an added attraction to what I do with Terry. That's the most important thing in my life. I know group things are a great recreation, and I understand that they're fine if you have an agreement in terms of the health things that are going on. But I couldn't be happy with just this, the way some guys are."

I felt a strange pang inside my chest when Luis said that. I tried to ignore it. I didn't even answer his question.

"There are some of the guys," he continued, "who explain that this is what sex is for them: the intense physical reality of men together. I guess it's just my Latin blood that makes me want to have romance and all of the rest of it also added in. I can strip down and get down just as well as the others, but I want my quiet times with Terry as well."

"Yeah," I finally admitted. "I understand." I did, all too well.

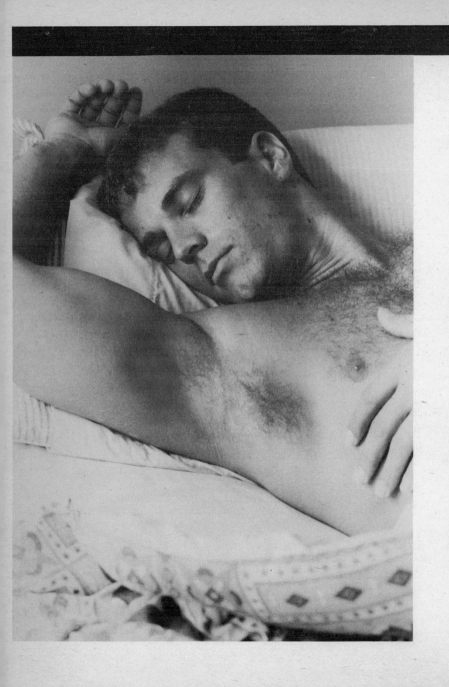

CHAPTER NINE

SOME QUIET TIMES

"Mr. Swann, don't you think that your overtly erotic performances only reinforce the idea that gay men are only interested in sex?"

I could barely make out the reporter's face through the bright lights of the news conference. I sensed that she was trying to trip me up, but I wasn't sure how, or why.

"No. I think it affirms an idea that gay men began with: that sex should be integrated into life in an open and honest fashion."

"But, Mr. Swann, you do, after all, focus all attention on your body. . . ."

"And on caring, taking responsibility for your own health, being open to relationships, all the rest of it."

"But AIDS is spread through sex."

"It's spread through irresponsible or uneducated sex. Its existence doesn't mean that we are supposed to suppress our natural desires or never enjoy sex again. It just means that we *all* have to be even more careful than we have been about how we have sex and under what circumstances."

"What do you mean by 'all'? Are you suggesting . . ."

"I'm saying that all sexually active people should be taking precautions in this day and age, regardless of gender. One of the messages I have to fight to get across is that this isn't something that only gay men get or that only homosexual men can give to one another.

"That's one of the things I have to protest about the press coverage of this epidemic. You keep on talking about it being a 'gay plague.' It's not. It's happened to gay men first in this country, as it turns out, but in other parts of the world AIDS is a heterosexual disease. One of the unfortunate results of this media bias is that all those men who have sex with other males and then go home to a wife or who have sex with many men and many women have this false impression that they can't be exposed—or can't expose others—in the heterosexual relationships. That's just not true.

"I think it's up to you people to start spreading that word. If you really want to help stop the spread of AIDS, then you should all have your newspapers begin a campaign to encourage the universal use of condoms. I know that wouldn't solve all the problems, but it sure would go a long way in helping the situation."

As soon as I stopped, questions were fired at me from the rows of chairs. After a while, I'd learned, you get to anticipate what reporters will ask you. It often made dealing with the press boring, but I also had learned what was needed from me to assure that the safe-sex movement got good press: The press had to have a smiling face that would look good on the television screen or in a newspaper photograph; a quick answer to their questions so they wouldn't waste their videotape, no four-letter words—please; and if you had to be sexually explicit, it was best to try to use medical terms if at all possible.

Formula, formula, formula!

The whole thing seemed to be becoming a prepackaged, flash-frozen series of repetitive slogans. As I was being carted around from city to city, pulled out to talk to reporters, dragged from club to bar to theater, my head would spin. Was this my clean jockstrap? Well, the laundry was done on Monday, so this must be Toledo!

All the cities and places had begun to blur.

Where was this press conference being held? Oh, yeah, Chicago.

"Pretty bushed, huh?"

I looked up at the Asian guy standing in front of me while a crew took down the television lights. The press conference— at least this one—was over.

"Yes," I admitted. His question brought me out of a daze, back to life. As I gathered up some papers I could see the group of people standing by the doorway waiting for me.

"You're keeping a heavy schedule."

"Sometimes it seems as if some people think this is only a game."

"Oh, Marty? Don't worry about her. She was checking you out for herself more than anything else."

"What do you mean?"

"She wanted to make sure you'd wear a rubber if she got you into bed. As soon as she heard your little rap about that, she started smiling. You went on her list of possibles." I stared at him.

"She's actually a bear about that—making sure that men use condoms." he went on. "Once she did a story on why there was so little disease among city prostitutes. She discovered that it was strictly a case of peer pressure. The old pros teach the new girls that there is one rule above all: All the johns use rubbers.

"That got Marty started. She became an evangelist in the studios, demanding that everyone—male and female—have his or her male partner use prophylactics. For a while she even started handing them out at the studio. After this afternoon I'll bet she goes out and has a T-shirt like yours made for herself: 'Ms. Safe Sex.' "

"Actually, it's not a bad idea."

"Marty has a lot of good ideas."

"You know her well?"

He suddenly grew sheepish. "She used to be my wife."

"Oh." It wasn't until that moment that the guy had made me forget my fatigue. He was a good-looking and (from what I could see through his clothes) well-built man. His hair was much longer and thicker than I was used to seeing, at least on the beaches back home, falling down over his shoulders. His mustache was bushy enough to match the heavy mane on the top of his head. The color of all that hair was an iridescent coal-black. But a man who had been married . . .

His announcement surprised me—and left me a little disappointed. I'd been hoping—but now that wasn't possible. Or was it? I felt unsteady, the swirl of emotions going on inside me was completely unfamiliar.

"Yeah, I used to swing that way a lot," he admitted. "I like women, though these days I head in other directions a lot more."

Now I wondered what he was really saying. Was he, in fact, suddenly available? I eyed him, still sitting in the chair I'd made my speech from. A technician came up and began to take away all the various wires that had been attached to me during the conference. When he was done, I was suddenly free from the restraints. But that liberty seemed only to add to my confusion.

I stood up, feeling awkward. I finally had enough sense to put out my hand, "You know my name, but I . . ."

"Yato," he said, taking my outstretched hand. His touch

was firm, and the shake seemed to linger half a beat longer than it really had to—but I wasn't about to complain.

"I hear you're doing a tour of the bars tonight."

"Yes. One of the local AIDS groups organized it."

"Do you get tired of it all?"

"You mean the publicity and the appearances?" *Or what else?*

"Yes. It must be difficult. I told you before, you look bushed. I doubt it's purely the physical exhaustion. This kind of work puts other demands on you, too. High stress."

"You're right. I really don't have much training for this kind of thing. To be honest with you, I wish the press would be interested in other people. I wish there were enough others who would be willing to lend a hand."

"Oh, the way you go at it, I bet you'd be in the fray even if there was an army of other people doing this work. I can tell when someone really believes in what he's doing. It's something you learn when you've been a reporter as long as I have." Suddenly he changed the tone of the conversation. "But I also bet you're not getting the kind of emotional support you need to be able to continue the pace you've set."

"I'm not quite sure what you mean. I have a good network back in Florida, and the people I meet are nice enough. . . ."

"But that real support is over a thousand miles away. What you're doing is going on right here." He reached out and put a hand on my elbow. It was such a small and subtle touch, so different from the sexual moves I was accustomed to. "Who's taking care of Glenn Swann these days?"

Suddenly I couldn't quite find my voice. It was somewhere down inside me, but I didn't know quite how to reach it.

"Your published schedule says you have a layover here in

Chicago tomorrow night. It's not much time, but how about letting me do some nice things for you?"

I nodded in agreement. I wanted that. Suddenly I felt exhausted. This kindness only made me realize how my energy had simply depleted. *Who's taking care of Glenn Swann these days*? That was an awfully good question.

"What hotel are you staying at?" I told him the name and he knew of it. "I'll pick you up at seven o'clock. All right?"

"Perfect."

Just knowing that Yato and I were going to get together made the rest of my schedule go more easily. I was smiling again, and once more feeling positive about the words I was speaking. I wondered just why this had happened. Why was I having this instant reaction? There had been so many people who'd been so kind, but now this one person was having a much greater impact than all the others put together.

Later on that night I was giving one of the parts of my rap that I most believe in, and I suddenly heard my own words: "Guys, we used to think that the only way to do it was to get it hard and shove it in something. That's not the way it goes anymore. It's something we're going to benefit from learning about, something that we probably should have figured out a long time ago. There's more to sex than getting it stiff and getting it off. There's caring about your body and taking responsibility for your own health. . . ."

I kept on speaking, but something told me that I had gone into automatic pilot. True, I meant all of my words. Yet I had forgotten to remind myself that the words I spoke were ones I had to internalize as well.

Of course, I'd had good sex on the road. Of course, I enjoyed the group at Terry and Luis's. Of course, I got off on playing the military drill instructor to Don—it still gave me a hard-on to remember that one in particular. But I hadn't *slowed down.* I'd allowed Karl to give my body pleasure, and I'd learned a lot about my physical responses from other men. But in the past few months, I still hadn't looked for something else, something more. I'd been too busy to let anything real happen, and it had been so long that I wasn't even sure what was real anymore.

I do know that when I got back to my hotel room that night and found a dozen red roses waiting for me, I felt like a teenager.

"Till tomorrow night," the card read. It was signed, "Yato."

I picked them up and pressed them into my face. *Flowers!* Butch, tough, in-command Sergeant Swann gets *flowers*?! And likes them? You bet he did.

Yato's work at the television station must have given him some inside connections at the hotel, because the flowers weren't the only little gift he was able to sneak into my room. His job must have also given him a lot of insight into what public people on tours must go through when they lead an existence of room-service meals, I soon discovered.

Usually in the mornings I have only juice and fruit for breakfast. I don't like to eat a lot when I know I'm going to work out, and the mornings were the only time I got to do that while I was on the road. But the day after the flowers arrived, a tray was delivered to my room. This time there was a single yellow bud on it—and another note.

Yato seemed to follow me wherever I went, not physically but with small messages and gestures. It was strange; such consideration was totally different from the sexual attention I was so used to receiving. I wasn't just being seduced, I realized—I was being courted.

The next day it all came to a head. I opened the door, and Yato was there, as he'd promised. He had already sent up enough flowers, so now, instead of roses, he carried a bottle of Dom Perignon in his hand.

I invited him in and was about to close the door when I realized that there was someone else besides Yato standing there. Yato was nothing if not thorough. Room service had already been called—he had obviously coordinated his arrival with theirs—and now a pair of waiters brought in a formal bucket and crystal glasses for the champagne, as well as an already set table of hors d'oeuvres.

I stood with my mouth open as the group of them went about the business of setting everything up. Yato was opening the wine as the waiters checked the details of the table. And I was . . . the object of all this!

In a matter of minutes the people from room service were gone and I was left with Yato. He handed me a glass of champagne. "To a restful evening," he said, a twinkle in his eye.

I took the glass from his hand and we sat down on the big, over-stuffed couch. I was just going to go along with whatever he planned, I decided—however he'd planned it. We began with small conversation. I learned the brief facts about his background. He's been born in Illinois, not far from Chicago. He'd attended local schools and colleges and gone into media work.

Soon he'd met Marty—the contentious reporter at the news conference—and they'd fallen in love. But from the start they'd had problems. Unsure of the sources of their difficulty, they just knew that they were unhappy. It didn't make a lot of sense; they knew they liked each other. Eventually, after a lot of painful arguments and hurtful acts, they realized that each of them had a sexuality that just wasn't going to work in a monogamous relationship.

"Of course, our timing was off. It was way, *way* off. We both wanted to be sexually active, but it wasn't the Age of Aquarius anymore." Yato shrugged and smiled at his own dilemma.

"How did you handle it?"

"We both agreed that the only thing to do was to sign up for the safe-sex movement. That's why I told you Marty was so adamant about it all. We . . ." Yato seemed to go away for a minute, as though he were weighing his next statement and what I'd think about it. He finally decided to go ahead. "We still sleep with one another. I told you: We like each other, a great deal."

"But you're divorced."

"Yes. We are divorced, but it didn't kill everything between us. We're still each other's best friend, and we still enjoy each another's company—and sex. That did make the safe-sex issue even more paramount in our minds, though. By then we were both being open about my attractions to men. I came out late—I waited until I was nearly thirty— and I didn't go through the bar scene very well. It didn't meet my own needs for affection and, well, romance. But, even just having a series of boyfriends and even one man I'd call a lover meant that I was having sex with more than a few males and . . .

"I know that this isn't going to sound quite right, but I'll say it anyhow, since it's the truth for me: If I was having sex and I was the only person I was putting at risk, I don't know if I'd be so adamant about safe sex. But I was coming back to Marty and—for a while—I was coming back to Jeff, my lover. I know, from what you've said at the press conference and other places, that you think we have what you call 'responsibility for our own health.' I understand that. But when there's the responsibility for others involved as well, when there are specific people that you love, then the requirements for being responsible are—for me—even greater. I can risk some things, but I have no right to force other people to risk them also, especially without their agreement or knowledge.

"But enough about me. By now you should have satisfied all your requirements for checking me out."

"What do you mean, 'checking you out'?"

"Isn't that part of it? Knowing what your partner's sexual habits are?" Yato reached over and ran one of his fingers over the side of my temple.

With that big, bad Sergeant Swann blushed. I shrugged a little bit. "I wasn't sure you were a bona-fide sexual partner."

"Oh, I think you can make that assumption." He leaned over now and kissed me softly. "Let's make Sergeant Swann feel good."

Assuming he meant that we should start having sex, I was all ready to unzip my fly. But he reached down and brought up one of the hors d'oeuvres. He put it to my lips, intent on providing for all the pleasures and needs a person might want.

After I'd eaten, we kept on talking for a while. We spoke about small, inconsequential things. I discovered myself reliving boyhood memories that I had all but forgotten. I described my life, and its ups and downs, to Yato.

He listened to every word. As I talked, his finger would move lightly over the surface of my flesh. It was a small but very comforting sensation. I would lean into his touch, moving my head to the side to have his palm rest against my cheek. Sometimes I wouldn't be willing to let my lips abandon the minute caress of his fingertips, and I would follow them when he tried to move them away.

I was as hard as a rock almost from the start. But my erection wasn't accompanied by the usual demands for instant gratification. Instead it was just a part of me that was reacting to Yato. Through it all he would continue to pour more champagne, feed me small pieces of food, and listen.

I'm still not sure if I could ever tell you which single thing was the most pleasant. It all came together to be an intensely satisfying whole.

"I'm proud of you for not calling me a geisha," he said at one point, smiling. "It seems as though all Anglo men think that any gentleness on the part of a Japanese must be from that tradition. They don't realize that such behavior could be something else: the understanding that all of the senses can be interlocked. There's nothing about being a man or a woman that makes one a better lover or a better provider to the sensibilities. We all have the capacity if we choose to express it."

"What do you choose to express now?" I asked.

"I express a desire to take you to one of the finest restaurants in Chicago where I can watch the waiters make fools over themselves when they see you walk in. I want to see the looks on the faces of all those women and men who think I am the luckiest person in the world because I have you by my side."

"That sounds like an expensive desire."

"Not nearly as much as you deserve. But come, let's go. I've made reservations for us."

We went to a bistro very close to my hotel, just off State Street. I tried hard to imagine someplace more romantic, but I couldn't come close to the small restaurant where the staff all spoke with authentic French accents and paid strict attention to every detail—including privacy when it was called for.

Yato was clearly in charge of this operation and went so far as to take the only menu and order for both of us. There was endless champagne. I sat there and drank it all in. Being such a focus of this man's concern and affection, I was actually just getting off on the extremes to which he was willing to go in this courtship.

Looking at him, I remembered all the articles I'd read

about safe sex and the rebirth of romance. I hadn't really gotten into that or paid much attention to it. "Dating" didn't seem quite my speed at the time. But this was the real thing—and I was enjoying every moment of it.

When we walked back to the hotel, we passed a few people on State Street. I couldn't quite understand why they were staring at us. Was it simply because one of us was Caucasian and the other Japanese? I was so into the mood that Yato had created that I didn't realize they were looking at the way he had his arm around my shoulder, or how I'd rest my head there every once in a while. In fact, I was so happy with this gentle moment that I didn't even care if we were creating a scene.

The uniformed elevator man didn't seem to mind, either. We fell into an embrace and a long kiss in the car as it went up to my floor.

I used the key to open the door to the room. As soon as it closed behind us, Yato's arms went around me again. He pulled me close to him, managing to maneuver me toward the bed. Before I knew it, I was sprawled out on top of the mattress.

He took off my shoes, then my socks. I helped him get my slacks and underwear over my hips. He had to lift up the top half of my body to remove the shirt. It was clear that he wanted to do all the undressing. I wasn't about to argue or resist.

When I was naked, I expected him to simply undress as well. But he only took off his jacket and shoes. He took me in his arms, and I could feel his strong, lithe body underneath the fabric. The juxtaposition of my nudity against his clothing was strange—and strangely exciting.

He was on top of me; his hands moved downward, onto my thighs and hips, reaching behind to grab my ass. A finger moved just as lightly and just as delicately through the cleft of my buttocks, as it had earlier touched my face. He leaned over, and I felt one of my nipples being sucked into his mouth. He rolled it over his teeth very gently.

I responded almost out of desperation. I wanted him badly. I kept trying to lift his head up to mine, but he'd fight it off and insist on keeping his lips on my chest. I wanted him to follow up the exploration in my ass—but he wouldn't move beyond his subtle caresses.

I could only manage to get my hands on some of his clothing. I unbuttoned his shirt first. His skin was extraordinarily smooth. He muscles were so tight that I could feel the thin layer of his skin barely covering them. There was only a small bit of hair on the parts of his body I could reach—just wisps under his arms.

I could have fought harder, I know that. I could have turned this into sexual combat just the way Zack had managed to transform our sex. But I was entrapped in our romance. I didn't want to break this mood at all. I wanted all the attention I was getting, and I didn't want to change the way things were happening one bit.

As he moved, his cloth-covered legs spread my knees apart. I could feel the hard flesh in his crotch as it pressed on me. His arms moved around my shoulders now. My nipple was finally free from the loving assault it had been receiving, and his lips were on mine. At last I was able to have his naked chest against my own.

Finally he let me remove his shirt. When he had to move a little bit to allow me to pull off his sleeves, he sat up, the two hard halves of his ass trapping my cock between them. I knew he could feel it. When the shirt was gone, he didn't move to come back to me.

While I was left with my hands reaching up to feel the broad and well-defined chest, he took off his belt and unzipped his slacks. Reaching down, his hand went inside his underwear. Even in the dimly lit room I could see the outline of his hard cock and the wet stain of his precum on the white cotton.

As I watched, he used the back of his hand to force the elastic band of the underwear down over his erection. His cock came out into the night, and the glistening drops that proved he was as excited as I was caught the little bit of light. I could see the drops where they had escaped from the slit at the head of his cock.

He moved forward, but he wasn't trying to reengage me in our embrace. Instead he ran his cock over my chest, letting it move through my hair and rubbing the wet and sticky tip over each of my nipples.

He stood up then and pulled off his slacks. Before he tossed them over to the nearby chair, he reached into the pockets where I could see that he'd kept two condoms.

Unwrapping one of them, he slowly and elegantly unrolled it over his own hard cock. With his tawny-colored erection now in an alabaster cloak, he moved to climb back up on top of the bed. This time when his hard ass touched me, it was resting on my thighs.

Then he took the second prophylactic and I watched, mesmerized, while it stretched downward to cover my own cock. The white latex seemed to be almost fluorescent in the night light. We were both so hard, the plastic was tautly pressed over our flesh.

He used his fingers to gently play with my cock again. This time his other hand went underneath and cupped my balls. I spread my legs farther apart for him, wanting to make sure there wasn't any hindrance to whatever explorations he might want to make.

I was expecting to get fucked. I thought that all of that caring he had shown me had to be something that needed to be paid for. I also assumed that the condoms were being put on in anticipation of that.

But Yato kept up his manipulations of my cock with his hand. He would roll my balls in his palm at the same time as he'd occasionally lean down and touch some other part of my body with his lips. To my surprise that was the extent of his attentions.

I felt myself beginning to come, waiting for the stuff to pulse out of me. My hips started to heave involuntarily; there was no way I could keep them still in the middle of all of this.

Then he stopped! Suddenly he stood up, his proud penis spearing the air in front of him. Smiling, he went back to the champagne cooler where the stoppered bottle was still on ice. He took out the temporary cork and filled two more glasses. I had my hand on my hard cock, that old part of me just wanting to jerk it off, but I wouldn't give into it. I wanted him beside me.

When he brought it over to me, I nearly refused the glass. Yet his smile reminded me of just how wonderfully things were going. "Relax, Glenn," he said softly. "Let it take a long while. You're going to be traveling again soon, and we might not see each other for a long, long time. I want you to remember this."

He reached over and let a bit of his champagne roll out of his glass and onto my belly. I stiffened quickly from the sudden cold but somehow managed to keep myself from actually jolting because of the sudden touch. A puddle of the sparkling wine was left in my navel. Yato leaned down and drank it out.

Then he took my latex-wrapped cock and held it on the edge of his glass. He tilted it so the head reached into the wine. Then he sucked the liquor off my cock.

All my mind could register was the idea of a slow, delicious, long time. And that's what we had together.

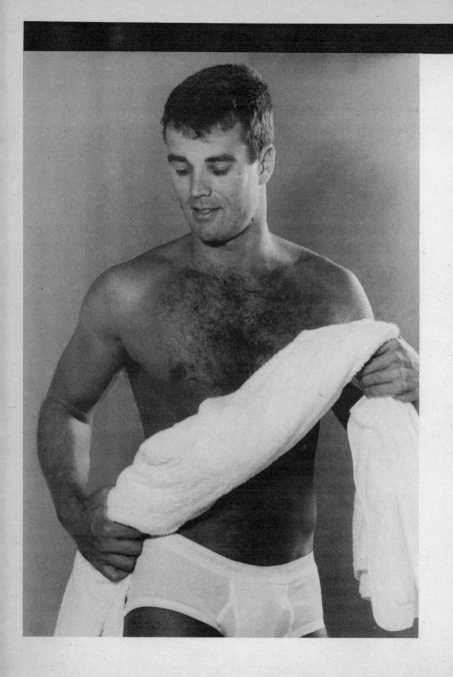

CHAPTER TEN

A VERY PRIVATE PERFORMANCE

My mid-continent tour ended in a few more weeks. That meant that my affair with Yato was going to end as well.

We'd maintained the romance with constant phone calls and frequent visits. I became an expert at manipulating airline schedules. I could figure out ways to fly to Chicago after the last of my shows and still meet my next day's obligations.

Still, we both understood that the pace couldn't be maintained, especially not after I left the same region and moved on to the West Coast. We agreed not to become maudlin. I thought that I might be acting somewhat cold about everything, but it did seem to me that the romantic interlude was just that—an interlude. We had never talked about the kind of love that leads to the monogamy that hadn't worked for Yato and Marty. But I shouldn't have worried. He was the one who finally cleared the air.

"Glenn, this is a wonderful way of relating, and it is something that I enjoy immensely, but I have to make sure that you don't misunderstand my intentions."

He was talking to me in an elegant Spanish restaurant

we'd found in Minneapolis. He'd flown up for the weekend to see me. The fact that he'd taken the trouble to do that made me well aware of all the caring involved.

"I really am not prepared to take on a committed relationship," he went on. "We're too old to be thinking in terms of leaving our own private worlds and putting the load of all those expectations on each other. We should know better. Not that it means I don't have many, many emotions about you . . ."

"And I have them for you, Yato," I said. "I know what you're trying to say. I have to admit I'm relieved that you're saying it. Honestly I am. I have to keep my promises and go on to the Coast. I know you have a career in Chicago and, well, our future plans just aren't going to mix well. I don't feel good about it. I wish things could work out otherwise, but I've known all along that it wasn't going to be permanent."

"I've thought about this a lot, you know." He was looking at me through those almond eyes. "I enjoy the affair so much, I wish we could leave it just at this level. I'm not sure why it either *has* to move on to something more inclusive or else simply end."

"I'm not sure what you mean, Yato."

"Glenn, why does something that gives two people great pleasure have to change? Why can't we just continue at this level? I wonder, sometimes, if my need for romance in my life—the image of a treasured person, the idea that there's someone there to send flowers to or receive a present from— isn't as honest as any other need. I think it might well be. I want to make a proposition to you."

"You're awfully good at those," I teased.

"I want us to continue to be special lovers to one another. Not 'lover' in the sense of married or even of boyfriends. Rather, loving people who make the gestures to one another that make life more enjoyable and who remind each other that we're remembered and special."

"But no strings? No future plans? What if there comes to be someone . . . more special?"

"Life has its tides, and the cast of characters changes for all of us. When that happens, then we'll move in other ways. We can always become friends—that's the most obvious option for us to consider now. Why not just let things happen and not force ourselves into decisions that aren't necessary, at least not yet?"

The rest of our night together was a little melancholy. We finished our meal and walked along the river. Stopping in a gay bar, we had a nightcap while we watched the stage show. Some people there had seen my own show earlier, and several of them came over to our table to introduce themselves.

They did it in the most friendly and accepting manner possible, but they also seemed to be a reminder that there wa an entire life I had that wasn't linked to Yato. It was something I believed in and wanted to continue, and it created other separations between us: the geography and time restraints that meant we couldn't take our romance to a conclusion that would have been an interesting route to travel, even if neither of us could say it was exactly logical.

Finally we got back to the hotel room. There we made the slow and familiar love we were used to. It was one of the things about our affair that I loved, but it definitely made things difficult, given the strain I was under with all the demands made on me every day. The truth was, our love-making took loo long. The entire evening could float by with constant caresses and a kind of sex that didn't seem to pay attention to the timing of an orgasm. Still, I knew that was only a small punctuation point in the physical communication we were involved in sharing.

We were able to spend most of the next day with each other. I had a couple of public appearances in the early afternoon and then one show early that night. I could watch

Yato in the audience. Every word I spoke, and all of the sexual gestures I made, were for him.

Afterward I had to take him to the airport. We weren't going to have much time, not only because of his flight, but also because I had to get to another performance in St. Paul, on the other side of the river.

When we said our good-byes in the car, I could sense a sudden playful mood in Yato. This was a different side of him than I'd seen before that weekend. I wondered what was going through his mind; he was so carefree all of a sudden, no longer worrying about the separation we were to go through.

"When you come to Chicago next week, I have a special favor to ask of you."

"Of course," I said. "I'd do anything you want."

"Fine." He smiled mysteriously. "I'll make all the arrangements."

I replayed that last conversation for the next week. As the flow of presents continued and the phone kept on ringing with news from him, I couldn't keep out of my mind the idea of the "special favor" I was going to be giving.

Was it sexual? I tried to think of something that we hadn't done with each other. After a week I simply couldn't come up with anything left—anything that two sane men would attempt, that is.

Did he want some other gesture? But what?

The next Saturday night Yato met me at O'Hare. I was free until I had to be in Louisville on Monday, so we had nearly forty-eight hours to accomplish whatever it was that he had in mind.

Obviously he had a plan, for he kept up the suspense. He wouldn't say a word about what he had in mind. We went back to his apartment on the north side of the city and made love. It was as quiet and as personal as ever. As usual, the followup after our orgasms was so gentle and peaceful that the line between consciousness and slumber was hard to define. I seldom remembered falling asleep when I was with him.

The next morning I woke up to the smell of bacon being cooked. Pulling on a robe, I got up. I walked into the kitchen to find him standing in front of the stove. He was naked. Walking up behind him, I put my arms around him, reaching down to cup the familiar cock and balls in my hands. I loved the pubic hair that surrounded them. It was straighter than either my own or that of other men I'd known, smoother and silkier.

He reached his head back and somehow managed to place a kiss on the side of my face. "Good morning," he said. I murmured something in reply. "I'm afraid you can't indulge in all of this right now. You need your strength. I've cooked one of your huge breakfasts for you. Go on, get over to the table and I'll get it ready."

It wasn't until I was halfway through the cup of coffee he'd given me that I was able to register what he'd said. "Why do I need special strength today?"

"The favor you're going to give me," he said. He placed a plateful of food in front of me and then went to pour orange juice for us. "You'll need *all* your stamina for it."

"Aren't you going to tell me about it?"

After he'd put the juice on the table he sat down. For a moment he seemed to be carrying on an internal debate while he weighed the question. "We both know that this part of our relationship is coming to an end. We've been through it all. We also agreed that we'd continue in our . . . special way. Well, I've come across a very obvious and unique fashion that will allow me to keep you a part of my life."

"I'm waiting, Yato. What is it?"

"I've arranged for the use of one of the studios at the station this afternoon. A good friend who's a technician has set up one of the cameras for me." I looked at him blankly. Where was this going? I wondered.

"I've always realized that I was lucky with you. Since I can find your picture in magazines, your image on commercial videotapes, I never have to go through feeling estranged not to have you close by. Sometimes the memory fails in certain ways; the details get lost, and what was so special, the little features, are forgotten. I didn't want us to go through that.

"When I was sitting in Minneapolis and watching you perform, though, I knew that you were really doing it *for me*. I've seen some of your theatrical tapes, and I've watched your show. You're very good at what you do. But, Glenn, they were done for everyone. Remember, I said I wanted to have you as a special person in my life and I wanted to be special for you.

"Last weekend the answer became clear.

"Here's the favor I want from you: I want to go to the studio this afternoon and I want to tape you myself. Just the two of us will be there; no one else will be around. You'll be performing for me. It's something that I know you'd do for me in the bedroom—we've done similar things with each other already. But this time it will be on tape and I'll be able to play it back whenever I want—or need that token of your presence."

It took me only a second to agree. "We'll make it into a special sex act between ourselves today," I answered. "I admitted to you I was able to get into being Mr. Safe Sex because I had my own pleasure in exhibiting myself. I went to a drama coach once—Larry, I told you about him—and he warned me that one of the things I'd have to learn was to remember to make my performances very personal.

"I use that advice a lot. This will be even more intense, Yato. If I'm doing a tape for you . . . well, it will simply be a far more serious performance than people usually think of erotica being."

"How do you feel about it being 'between us,' though?" he asked.

I smiled, just bashful enough to look away from his gaze as I gave the details. "I want you to talk to me while it's going on. I want you to feed into my liking to show off. You can help me make this something that we'll both remember for a long time."

"I get your videotaped performance if I give you the dirty talk to go with it? Remember, Glenn, this is actually one of the last times we'll see each other for a while. It's an opportunity," Yato said. "We can not only provide the record for me but also make sure that we have a really special sexual event to remember. The studio's waiting, let's do it!"

Soon I stood in front of the lights, staring into the eye of the camera that was trained on me. Using all of Larry's teaching, I kept in mind that the machine wasn't simply an impersonal, mechanical device. It was the extension of this loving man, Yato. I was not performing for a detached audience; I was performing for him.

We'd agreed on the way it would be done. I was going to go through the acts that he requested, just as we'd do if we were in bed together. I'd add what I wanted to give him, presents of sheer pleasure from me to him. The voice from the camera would keep talking to me while I performed; it would remind me of who I was and who was watching.

I had on street clothes. This wasn't a performance by Mr. Safe Sex; I was just Glenn Swann. There was a very simple set: a double mattress made up with sheets and blankets on a platform only a few inches higher than the floor.

If Yato hadn't been there, I would have felt my usual awkwardness. But I was already in the mind-set that told me this was an intimate affair between the two of us. This was *our* sex.

"Undress for me, Glenn." His face was behind the camera, but it made his presence real. "Do it slowly. Let me watch every part of you. Strip for me."

"Where do you want me to begin?" I asked. I had my hands on my waist, my legs spread apart. "What would you like first?"

"Your shirt. Let me see your chest. I want to think about that."

I reached down and took the bottom hem of my shirt and pulled it slowly up from the belt.

"Your stomach is perfect. I remember putting my head on it in bed last night and feeling the pulse of your arteries. I could hear you then." His voice had an excited tone to it, as if he were whispering in my ear.

The shirt traveled farther up. I could feel a slight draft on my nipples as the cloth uncovered my pectorals. "Yes, those little things. Every time I kiss them, you shudder a little bit. Not much—but enough that I can remember how important they are to you."

My arms lifted the shirt so high now that it covered my face. But rather than complain about that, Yato talked about the other parts of me that were now exposed. "I love your armpits. The way the hair curls there in the deep cavity when you sweat and the sharp aroma that rises up from them when you work out."

The shirt was gone now. I tossed it aside. "Stand there. Don't move! I'm coming in closer. Now I'm looking at your tits again, remembering the lines around them and the way they stand up when you get excited. The camera's moving up, Glenn, to your neck. Turn your head . . . yes, yes, that's it! Let me see the muscles on the side of it. Yes. Good. Now make your arms move so the muscles will stand out and I can see the lines of them."

I turned to show about a half profile to the camera. I grabbed my wrist with my other hand and applied as much tension as I could. I got another yes from Yato.

"Please, Glenn." His voice had a small hint of sexual urgency now. "Please, undo your pants while you're standing that way. Slowly . . . very slowly. I'm moving in so I can imagine the smell of you, as though my face were right beside you."

I did it as deliberately as I could. I forced my mind to

remember how much I would enjoy undoing each one of Yato's pants buttons. I let the denim fall apart, forming a wider triangle of white as more of my shorts was exposed. When my jeans were so far opened that they couldn't keep up the tension and slipped over my hips, I let them drop to the floor from their own weight.

"Stop! Stay right there. You look as if you're a young man who's been trapped in the act of undressing. It's even more sensual, more erotic, than usual."

I looked right into the camera. I knew, though, that the lens wasn't focused on my face. I could *feel* it staring into my crotch in the way a passionate lover would. I could feel more than just that. I could sense my blood flowing into my cock. The soft flesh was becoming excited and rigid, responding to the attention it was getting, enjoying the verbal lovemaking as much as it might savor the actual physical touch.

"Now, Glenn, take off your shoes. No, wait! Turn around. Let me watch you from the back while you bend down. Yes, yes, like that. I want to see the way your ass presses against the white shorts. I can see the dark line down the middle, the place where so much is hidden. When you bend over this way, I can actually look into you and see the hair that's gathered around there. . . .

"I'm moving in with the camera. It would love to fuck you, Glenn. I'd like to take the lens right up your asshole. I'd love to! I'm moving down now, inside your legs. I'm up to the back of your knees. That's your secret place, isn't it? I'll always remember the way you respond when I touch you there.

"And your calves! You've been working on them in the gym, haven't you? I know you have. I just know it. They look so starkly muscled when I see them this way. I can define the parts of your leg as well as I could on a chart. Beautiful, Glenn. It's just beautiful.

"Now, turn around to face me again. Yes. That's better.

Spread your legs. Stand the way you were in the very beginning with your legs far apart and your hands on your waist. That's it. Look how big your cock's gotten. Just from me talking to you? Is that it? Or is it the idea that I'm going to be able to see you like this whenever I want to? I'll only have to turn on a video recorder. It will be like our other times together.

"I'll be sipping champagne and holding my hard cock, watching yours grow from the excitement, and I'll be able to know that it's me that caused it. Rub your hand there, feel what effect I have on you, Glenn. Grab hold of your own physical strength and understand that I'm the one who can bring it to life, make it so powerful."

I rubbed my hand over my erection, feeling it through the cotton. The cloth was thin and light, but it began to feel like some kind of amazing bondage, forcing me to restrain myself.

"Do you want to take it out for me, Glenn? No! Don't do it yet. Answer me first. Do you want me to see it?"

"Yeah." I was surprised by the deep huskiness of my voice. "I want you to look at my cock."

"Then do it slowly, Glenn. Very, very slowly. Show me the tip first. Only the hard top of it where the knob is so big and the skin is such a dark and violent purple. Yes. That. That's what I want to see. Let it slide up over the waistband, just that part of it.

"Now let the tight elastic run down the length of the rest of you. Yes, yes, let it all come out into the open. Let the air on it. I'm close up, Glenn. I can see every inch of your veins along the surface. They're such dark, violet ridges against your pale white skin.

"Let the elastic slip beneath your balls now. Yes, that's it! Hold it right there. You're offering them up to me now, Glenn, as if they were on some kind of platter, waiting for my tongue to move in and wash them, rinse off every drop of the salty sweat on them. . . .

"Push the shorts off, Glenn. Stand totally naked in front of me with your hard cock pointed at the camera. Hold it by the base and let it swing free and hard, as though it were teasing me, inviting me to come over and slip a tight condom over it."

I felt my throat contracting while all this was going on. I wanted Yato to be here, not behind a camera. I wanted the touch of his body next to mine. I wanted to feel his smooth skin. . . .

"Play with your tits, Glenn. Get yourself hot for me. Do it the way I would if I were there myself. Wet one of your fingers and let it glide over the surface. Is the flesh there getting harder?"

"It's as hard as my cock." It was; I was telling the truth.

"Stand sideways again. Let me see how long and stiff your erection is. Lift up your balls again, just with your hand, so I can see all of them from here. Don't move for a moment; I want to have a long, long exposure of this. . . .

"Move now. Turn around. Let me see the back of you without even the shorts to conceal any of it."

I was feeling the camera again. I still could hear Yato as he spoke, describing every inch of my body. I almost didn't need the reminder of his presence. I could sense the way the camera was roaming across my shoulders. I could imagine his hands exploring the parts of me that the camera was recording.

"Glenn, get down on your knees. That's right, stay facing away from me. Yes, like that, but spread your legs, give your balls room to swing back and forth. Lean forward, Glenn, all the way. Put your head and shoulders on the mattress and leave your buttocks spread apart that way. This is the best view, Glenn. I can see the whole back of your balls; I can watch the line of skin that divides them and then moves up that small part of the body between your balls and your asshole. It just dives into it, disappearing into that hair-protected cavity.

"Doesn't it feel empty without me around? Don't you want my cock up there?"

"Of course I do, you bastard!"

"Then open it farther. Come on, get your knees farther apart so that there's no flesh covering you up. I want to see you more naked than any other man ever has. Does it make you horny to show it off to me, Glenn?"

"Yes!"

"So horny you want to beat off?"

"You know I do. Yato, I'm already dripping onto the sheet; that's how hot I am."

"Go on, then, do it. Don't change your position! Stay right there. I want to watch your testicles bouncing up and down as you jerk your cock off. Yes! That's it. I'm coming back in for another close-up. I can watch the small, hairy eggs of yours jumping in their sac. Do you want to come, Glenn?"

"Yes, please, Yato, let me . . ."

"No! Not yet. Roll over, let me watch it. Keep your legs spread! Don't try to hide your balls after all this. I can still see them. And now I have the bush of pubic hair on top of your cock as well. I can see the way it covers your belly. Now stop!"

He stepped away from the camera just enough to throw me a condom. "This has always been part of our sex, Glenn. I want to have you wear it while we do this part as well."

I took the wrapped prophylactic and opened it. I put it at the head of my stiff cock and—always aware of Yato's camera and always trying to make myself look as good as possible—I slowly sheathed my erection with it. It was white, growing translucent when I stretched it over my rigid flesh. We could both see the roundness of my veins and the ridge of my cock's head.

"Now, Glenn, beat it off. Make yourself come in the condom."

I obeyed. I took my hand and began to jerk off, using my

other hand to hold myself up. This position made the lines of my abdomen more pronounced, I knew. I kept looking down at the wrapped cock. My precum was trapped inside the latex. The lines of fluid were seeping along the sides. The pressure was building and building. The liquid was increasing in quantity.

"Come for me, Glenn. Shoot for me. Show me what it means to do this in front of the camera for me. Glenn, come on, shoot it . . . !"

My stomach cramped and my shoulders convulsed as the orgasm grabbed hold of my whole body. My legs buckled from the shock. The stuff just flew out of me, and the rubber expanded from the pressure of my ejaculation.

All I could do when it was over was collapse onto the mattress. My arms were above my head; my lungs were struggling to recapture my breath.

"Don't move."

I opened my eyes and saw that Yato was standing over me. His pants were open and his cock was hard and ready. He had the video camera slung over his shoulder. He somehow was able to manage while his free hand jerked himself off.

I saw his knees bending and recognized the sign that his orgasm was almost there. "I want this on you in the film, Glenn. I want this evidence that I've had you. . . ."

Then he shot too. His cum flew through the air and splattered on my chest, my belly, and even on my pubic hair. The liquid was warm when it first hit. That only seemed right—that it would be as hot as our passion.

When he was finally drained, Yato clicked off the camera and put the machine down on the floor. He laid his body on top of mine, not caring if his clothes picked up the fluids from our sex. He wrapped his arms and legs around me and we stayed there, just holding each other.

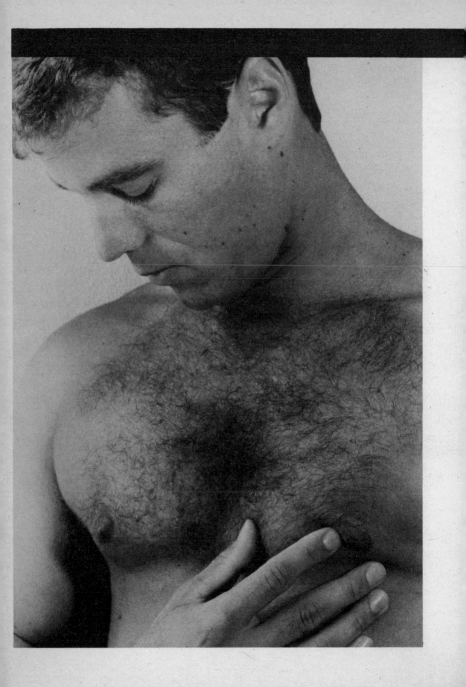

CHAPTER ELEVEN

A BIT OF SWINGING

I sat in the plane hurtling westward toward California. Yato was behind me, at least for now. I'd learned a lot in the time I'd spent with him, and the lessons had been on many different levels.

For one, I'd remembered how much I needed to take care of *all* my needs. The whole health crisis had made me think so much about the denied outlets for sex that I had forgotten that sex was never the only thing in life. I had emotional needs as well. They weren't going to go away because of a virus. In fact, if I didn't meet them, the stress that was going to result might even help weaken my energies in a way that invited the virus into my body.

The massage with Karl had been my first really overt move into the world of safe sex. It was, I realized now, a particularly appropriate one. Massage hadn't been merely a different way to have sex; it was also a way to force myself to take some time out, get some satisfaction for myself, make sure that the kinds of pressures I was putting myself under were relieved in many ways, not just orgasmically.

155

I had seen, once again, the capacity I had for romance. In the very beginning I had decided that I wasn't going to use the health issues to run into the arms of a love affair created only for the sake of security and some kind of guaranteed sex. But that didn't mean that I didn't want the option to accept it if it should come along.

It's amazing how important it can be simply to consider the possibility of romance. The idea alone cheered me up; it was a great feeling.

I thought about my last experience. My making the video-tape for Yato was something I could share with audiences in the future. I had heard from a lot of men that they had been used to being monogamous when their lovers were in town but had felt free to go roaming when their partners were away. Those had been the times they'd gone off to the bars or the baths.

True, they could still do that, limiting themselves to safe sex. But it obviously wasn't as free an alternative as it once had been. I knew that some guys, at least, had or could afford to get portable video machines that would produce tapes they could play on their home VCRs. What a great idea, I thought, to tape one another and then have the tapes as a source of companionship when lovers had to be separated!

If they didn't have the means to be that elaborate, there was a much less expensive option. I automatically touched my breast pocket and felt the small cassette that Yato had handed to me at the airport when he'd seen me off the last time. On it was the voice track from our session together. Whenever I wanted to have my own private time with him, I could just put it on a small recorder and play back the sound of his voice when I was alone at night and wanted to rekindle the memories of our time together.

Soon the flight attendants passed out soft drinks, inter-rupting my thoughts to tell us lunch was about to be served.

I was still in a dreamy state, happy to have the time during the flight to be alone with my private memories.

The woman beside me had other ideas, however. Her name, she informed me, was Linda. She was from the South, which had been obvious from her accent, and she was traveling on business. I, myself, generally enjoy being alone on long plane rides, but Linda was a friendly, vibrant person who was obviously more interested in a conversation than in her own privacy. Actually, a conversation was the least she was going to settle for, I discovered.

We talked about the small things that recent acquaintances share. Soon she was pressing me for more information. "What do you do for a living?"

"I'm an entertainer."

"Oh, really! Should I know you?" She obviously hoped that she had been seated next to someone whose name she'd recognize.

"I honestly doubt it."

"Now don't be so quick with your answer. I know a lot of people in the business. Are you a singer?"

'No, that's one thing I've never done."

"An actor?"

"Sort of." I was squirming in my seat a little bit now. I felt trapped by her questions; I really didn't want to get into a whole discussion on sexual identity with someone who could turn out to be very unhappy about her neighbor.

"Television!"

"I've done some." Well, I *had*! And recently too.

"What network?"

"Actually, my work's been limited to a small syndicate."

"Oh." She was clearly disappointed. Then a flight attendant came by. I seldom drink alcohol, but a cocktail suddenly seemed like a good idea at that moment. I quickly discovered that I'd made a miscalculation, though, as the drinks we got only warmed Linda up even further. As her questions kept flying in my direction, so did the rest of her attentions.

"Now, Glenn," she said with a smile, time to confess. "Tell me just what it is you do."

Her hand had moved to my thigh by now, and I wasn't sure if she was asking me what I did vocationally or . . . But my real dilemma was that I found myself responding to her. I had had relationships with women before I came out, especially when I was in the Marine Corps and I had enjoyed them a great deal. It was never a question of not liking women that led me to come out; I just liked men more. But I hadn't been involved with a woman in years. Still, that didn't mean that I was incapable of responding to Linda now.

Actually, she was quite beautiful. Her complexion was flawless. Her breasts were high and firm, which was obvious from her tight blouse. I think that Yato's stories about his wife, Marty, might have been influencing me as well. I remembered hearing him talking about the good sexual times they had together and secretly been a little turned on.

The vivid descriptions of how much Yato loved Marty's body had brought back my own bisexual memories. I would listen to him and think, Oh, yeah! That feeling! We had even become little boys at one point, acting as though we were in camp sharing our sexual secrets, talking not about one another's bodies, but about the things about women that we had liked the most.

There had been many things that I'd come up with—and Linda's presence was reminding me of them all. There's the soft skin and the wonderful curves. Just because a guy likes hard muscles doesn't mean he has to dislike the sight and feel of a woman's breasts.

I found myself slipping into some old habits and discovered that I wasn't just accepting Linda's small seduction, I was encouraging it.

But honesty . . . that was the thing that I had made such a central part of my life and my work. You have to be honest with people about yourself. I knew that one of the biggest problems with the health crisis came from people's refusal to deal with it and discuss their activities openly. Deceit was the partner in this crime.

In another time and place I think that I might have played along with Linda's come-ons. But I couldn't do it now. Finally I told her that she had to understand things about me. I said I was gay.

Much to my surprise, she turned out to be a very savvy woman. "Irrevocably?" She spoke without a hint of sarcasm in her voice. Her tone seemed to imply that she was willing to keep the subject open so long as I allowed a glimmer of possibility.

"Well . . ."

"Well, what? Are you *just* gay?"

"No. Yes. I mean . . . look, Linda. I'm *gay*, that's the life I'm in, and I choose to stay there. But I guess I'm not limited to sex with men, if that's what you're asking."

"That's all I'm asking." The hand went to my kneecap. "If I went around insisting that every man I met had to be a candidate for fatherhood and marriage, then I'd need a total background check. But when it's a question of a couple of people having a good time away from home—when they're both adults and their eyes are wide-open—well, that's a different story. The same rules don't apply. Now, tell me much more about yourself. Tell me the good stuff. What do you really do?"

There was nothing to be gained by hiding anything from her, so I told her all about the Mr. Safe Sex Tour I was doing. I might as well let her know now, I realized. There

was going to be a committee welcoming me at the Los
Angeles International Airport.

"Do you mean to say that the man I'm making eyes at on
this airplane is going to be greeted by a contingent of the gay
world when we get off the plane?"

" 'Fraid so."

"Well . . . stewardess! I think I need another drink over
here." After we'd gotten a couple more cocktails, Linda
starting laughing. "People will not believe this when I tell
them. Glenn, you are just my type—I thought you were—
you *look* like you're just my type. I guessed you'd been in
the Marines the minute I saw you, for one thing. But now I
find out you're a star in the gay world. Not just a gay man,
understand, but a damn star!"

We kept on joking, talking easily. As we relaxed, I realized that the warmth between us was picking up again. For a
while I thought that it was just the unaccustomed alcohol
taking effect. But the look in Linda's eyes was more than a
little friendly again.

A voice came over the loudspeaker, announcing that we
were making our final approach to LAX. The flight attendants took care of getting us ready to land. Then, after the
plane had touched down and was taxiing to the gate, Linda
leaned over to me. "Glenn, let's see each other while we're
in Los Angeles. I've never been here before. It's a dead
business trip for me, and I really could use someone to have
fun with. Tell me where you're staying."

We exchanged local addresses. I wondered whether or not
this was the best idea in the world. Wasn't life complicated
enough? With someone like Yato around, reminding me that
I might be getting myself involved in a single relationship
down the road, did I really want to consider getting involved
with both sexes? It was a question I wasn't sure I could
answer.

*   *   *

Two days later I found myself on the beach with Linda. My mind had continued the seemingly endless questioning after our trip to California. I had watched her amusement when a cadre of local activists had met me at the gate with a banner that read: WELCOME, MR. SAFE SEX! Perhaps, I thought, I was just some kind of oddity for her, something that she'd like to collect and brag about.

But my questions all melted away when she kept her promise and called me. I decided that I should be totally honest about everything and made sure that the description of my act was as complete as possible. I was pleased to find her listening eagerly for my description of the performance I'd given at a benefit the night before.

She loved it all, laughing with me when I described the effect a chilly breeze had had on me. Then she asked if I could manage to be free for the afternoon. She wanted to get some sun while we were in California, and this was the only day she had when it would be possible. Before I knew it, I heard myself agreeing.

Now we were on the beach. She was wearing a very slight bikini. The pants were two small triangles tied together with strings on the sides of her hips. Her bra was full with those wonderful breasts of hers. I caught myself studying them and the large nipples that pressed against the fabric.

I had on a pair of briefs. They were white; I'd just picked them up in the hotel lobby store on the way out here, since I hadn't brought any swimwear with me. Although I had wanted to go into the Pacific while I was here, I thought I could have gotten by with just some gym shorts.

After a while I left Linda to her sunbathing and went to the water's edge. The ocean was cold, but I was determined to go in, even if the other, more sane people were avoiding it. When I came back and began to dry myself off, I realized that Linda was studying me carefully.

"Talking to you opens up all kinds of possibilities for me, you know," she said.

"What do you mean?" I asked.

"I've never been to one of those places—Chippendales and clubs like it. But I've fantasized about them a lot. Now, here I am with you. When I get by the fact that you do it for gay men, I also remember that you're a stripper, at least in a sense. I wonder what it would be like to have a man perform that way. There are a lot of things that women don't get to experience sexually. That kind of show is certainly one of them."

"Want a show of your own?" I thought I was joking.

"Actually, I already had one!" She laughed. "When you just came out of the water, your suit became nearly transparent. Didn't you know that? I thought you did it on purpose. Every person on the beach could see through it when you walked back up from the shore."

I looked down and realized that the damp cloth was as revealing as a wet pair of jockey shorts would have been. There was hardly anything to keep the people around me from seeing every part of me—every inch.

I quickly sat down and put my towel over my crotch. Linda laughed more loudly now. "What's the big deal? You've just been telling me that you show it off to hundreds of men all the time."

"I choose to do that," I answered, angry at the way she was implying that I had no right to privacy. "There's a big difference."

"Hey"—she spoke softly now—"I'm sorry. I didn't mean to make you angry."

I shrugged to let her know the moment had passed and I was all right. In fact, I couldn't help breaking into a smile of my own at the idea of the unconscious strip I'd just performed. I wondered what some of the family groups around us had thought of it.

We passed the rest of the afternoon on the beach and then went to a restaurant nearby where there was great fresh seafood. As we ate abalone together we kept on talking about ourselves. I had a show to do; she had an early appointment. After we'd eaten, I drove her back to her hotel.

I can't honestly tell you if I was surprised that Linda was in the lobby bar of my hotel when I returned from the club where I'd been performing that night. I suppose I should say it was unexpected. We'd said our good-byes after a wonderful afternoon.

That, I supposed, was it: The afternoon had been wonderful. Just as I could feel the tightness on my skin from the exposure to the sun, I could feel the tightness in my body that she could evoke.

She and I looked at each other while I stood in the middle of the area and shook hands with the men who'd been my hosts. They had offered to take me to the bars, but I told them now that I was tired; I'd just stay here for the night, after all. I thanked them for their help, and we made arrangements for them to pick me up in the morning for another appointment.

I watched them leave the building, then I walked over to where Linda sat. After I ordered a glass of wine we talked a bit, as naturally as if we'd planned this all along.

"I don't know, Linda," I said after a while. "I feel strange about this. I mean, I'm not going to do anything more with you than this. . . ."

"Glenn, if you don't want me here, it's fine. I'm the one who decided to show up unannounced. But you've told me a lot about your sexuality. You certainly seem to be willing to go to bed with a lot of men whom you only expect to know that night. What's the difference here? We've been having a good time, and it just seems natural to me that it should continue a little bit longer—just for the night. I go back home tomorrow, no strings attached."

We eventually did go to my room. Once the door was closed, we kissed. I could feel the different body, smell the exotic odors, all of it so different yet so much of it the same.

I moved to reach up under her blouse. I felt her breasts— there was no bra to cover them underneath. Her skin was incredibly smooth and inviting. We moved toward the bed and fell on it, still in each other's arms.

The undressing and the lovemaking went on for a long time. I had a hard time letting my body just flow with the emotions and the physical stimulation. I was having sex with a woman again, and there was so much that rummaged through my mind about it.

Finally I was able to conquer all my various distractions; I told myself that I was *with Linda!* That's what was important. I had been having nothing but good sensations from the erotic interaction we'd had all day. But whenever I had slipped into that idea that I was with a woman—whenever I forgot that I was acting in my own personal manner with this one individual—I would have trouble maintaining an erection.

That made me self-conscious, but she didn't seem to care. Our hands and lips kept up their explorations, and her long nails continued to make their light scratches on my back, as though they could coax me even further into the desire we shared.

"Fuck me, Glenn," she finally whispered. "Come into me."

I stood up to go to my slacks where I knew there was a condom. She seemed to understand what I was doing. "You don't have to. I've taken care of that."

"Linda, it's not for the same reason."

She didn't argue with me, though she seemed surprised that I was actually putting the condom on. When it was ready, and while I was holding it at the base of my penis so it wouldn't slip, I moved back next to her and we began all over again.

I got rock-hard quickly. I moved in between her legs and felt myself enter the no-longer-familiar warmth of a woman's sex. She sighed, lifting up to meet me, wrapping her legs around mine.

As we moved together I was awed by the difference between being with her and with the men that I was more used to. It was more liquid, and there was less friction as well. The softness of her body was . . . different. That's really the only word to describe the physical part of it. But all the essential things were still there. I was with a person I liked, and we were celebrating our kinship with sex.

I rolled her over on top of me, which she obviously liked. She sat up, letting her large breasts swing over me, and reached down to feel my cock where it was encased in her wetness. Her fingers seemed to manipulate my erection, directing it to do more than simply thrust in and out of her. She wanted to feel it pressing against the sides of the lips and up against the top of the beautiful entry to her body.

I could feel a tightness coming from her now as the strong vaginal muscles began to clamp down on my cock. The surges of power that I was feeling coming from her seemed to be milking my orgasm from me. Even before I heard the deep and heavy breathing that announced her fall into ecstasy, my own stomach was pulling inward, the lines across it deepening as I felt my own fluids flow out of me. Afterward we lay stroking each other for a long time.

*   *   *

"You didn't have to use the rubber, Glenn. I'm surprised you did. Most men hate them."

"Linda, you've heard me talking about safe sex since we first met."

"But that's for men."

"No. I'm sorry. It's for all sexually active people. Especially men, perhaps, but certainly for men who've been with other males—no matter if they're with women at that moment. Your gender doesn't protect your health in this one."

"Well, you're the only guy I'd have to worry about," she said, kissing me on the cheek. "The rest . . ."

"You don't know about the rest of them. You really have got to realize that it was hard—even for me—to be honest with you about my sexuality when we met. It's not an easy thing for a person to open up about all the time. I wish it weren't the case, but there it is.

"Now, if *I* have a hard time talking openly about my gay life with a straight person, what about someone who's just had secret sex someplace—and he's really guilty about it? He's not going to own up to that information easily. Believe me, you have every right to explore all that healthy sexual interest of yours. There's definitely nothing wrong with that kind of erotic appetite. I'm sure it's better to be like us and to be open to new experiences than to deny them and try to keep them hidden away deep inside. But not everyone realizes that, and you just have to learn to protect yourself every way you can nowadays."

"What, should I walk around with a pocketbook full of condoms?"

"Hey, don't get angry with me. I'm trying to give you the best advice I can about all this. But you have to listen. And, *yes*, the answer is that you should always have prophylactics with you if you're even going to entertain the idea of being open to sex."

She giggled. "It reminds me of the boys in high school who would act so butch while they showed one another the rubbers they kept in their wallets. I suppose it's just another one of the signs of liberation—just a far different one than we thought we'd get.

"But I know you're right, Glenn. And I'm glad I met you." She leaned over and kissed me once more. "Not just because I enjoyed this tonight—which I definitely did. But I also needed to hear what you just told me. I guess I simply wanted to make believe that all of this was something of concern only to other people. I didn't want to have to face it myself. Now I know I have to. And let me tell you, it's a lot easier to hear this kind of news from someone you care about and someone who's shown you that he cares."

"Well, you're just going to have to become one of my new recruits," I said.

"What?"

"I have a little safe-sex army. In cities all across the country there are 'Mr. Safe Sex' guys just like me. There's even a woman in Chicago who's 'Ms. Safe Sex.' "

"Well, make me number two, then. I'll do my duty. My grandmother used to wrap bandages for the war effort; I guess carrying around condoms isn't much worse."

The next morning I sent a postcard to Yato. "You know, maybe you and Marty would enjoy that video together. Don't think I have any objections if it'd be something you'd like to share with your ex-wife and current lover!"

I was becoming quite the cosmopolitan!

CHAPTER TWELVE

CRUISING THE BARBARY COAST

Leave it to a trip to San Francisco to clear up any lingering confusion I might have about my sexuality! As soon as I got off the plane from Los Angeles and drove up the freeway to that city by the bay, I could feel the rush of gay urges coming over me.

Of course, the fact that the party greeting me at the airport was made up of contestants from a local gay body-building contest didn't exactly hurt.

I was sitting with four men who were so large that the five of us could barely be contained in the car. I kept on looking down at the enormous biceps on each side of me, wondering just what these guys did to keep in that kind of shape. I mean, I was careful about my body and kept up my workout schedule even while I was touring, but my arms weren't ever going to be that big—ever.

They dropped me off at a hotel downtown. I had a few hours before I was to show up to judge their competition, and while I unpacked, I wondered about the response I'd had to those men. I'd had two major adventures in the very recent past: a very important affair and a night with a woman. Did it only take a ton of beefcake to turn me back into a lusting gay man, ready for the fast lane in one of the sexiest cities in the country?

Well, it wasn't quite that simple. But as I undressed and got into the shower I realized that I was back to being what I wanted to be: Mr. Safe Sex spreading his message to the gay world.

Yato had been a special way for me to get personal support to balance the public life I led. I hoped he'd continue to be just that. But neither of us wanted him to be something that kept me from my work or my personal pleasure—and he wasn't going to be.

I was delighted with the time I'd spent with Linda, but it was hardly any indication that I was going straight. Everything was part of the learning experience, I decided. I could take back to my audiences everything I was going through as Mr. Safe Sex and share it with them, to let them know the safe ways in which they could still have active sex lives. We still have a lot of options, and we should indulge in all of them.

When I walked into the hall a short while later and heard the cheers from the crowd, I realized that no matter what personal gains and benefits I'd received from the past few weeks with Yato, I had also been rejuvenated by him. I was getting back into my life on the road in much better shape. True, I had appreciated what Linda had meant to me in our brief time together, but the priority I had in my life was right here in this room.

Right now the throngs of men, hyped up by the idea of the contest and the idea that I was one of the judges, was a big factor contributing to their energy level.

Mr. Safe Sex rides again!

The competition was being sponsored by a collective of

local gay health clubs in the city. It was one of the most unique I'd ever seen because it not only was truly a legitimate bodybuilding event—these guys were *built*—but it was an overtly erotic one as well.

The night started with the guys coming onto the stage in their street clothes. They all seemed to go for the Castro Street look, pure urban gay male; most of them had on flannel shirts or strap T-shirts, boots of some sort, and paper-thin jeans with faded areas (usually on their crotches) that looked suspiciously as though they'd been sandpapered to help the natural bleaching process.

Several men were more original in their costuming. The audience and I gave them a special applause when we saw them strut across the stage. One guy appeared in a leather outfit complete with a harness that crisscrossed his chest with leather bands and accentuated his huge pectorals.

Another arrived in a three-piece suit—that was a great favorite, especially when he removed the jacket and the crowd saw that his oxford cloth shirt was a fake. He wore only a bib to make it appear as though he wore a shirt, but his back and sides were naked. Two others favored uniforms, showing up as a cop and a sailor.

After the clothed presentation the guys went through a real routine. Each had chosen his favorite music and stood posing to its beat. Some of them were really artists at it, using a wide range of styles to their best advantage.

If I was taking my role seriously (along with the other judges), the audience's appreciation was far more direct. More than the typically appropriate response to a wonderfully built body, they also seemed to show some special added appreciation and applause for the display of a handsome face or in approval of a sly erotic gesture.

At last came the final act to the night's festivities. This was the "fantasy" segment of the show, the part of it that was the most overtly erotic. One by one the men came out in costumes designed to turn on the crowd—and themselves.

Every one of them—to a man—displayed his massively developed, naked buttocks. Each wore jockstraps, G-strings, or other kinds of posing straps. The fabric that covered their genitals seemed designed to hide as little as possible. If the crowd had been swayed by beautiful faces, it now proved itself capable of delirium over particularly well-exhibited sets of cocks and balls.

In this segment the contestants seemed much more liberated about their presentations. The emphasis tended toward movie fantasies with more than a few Conans. Others were candidates for gladiator movies, with metal bands around their biceps and foreheads and various ancient-seeming armaments in their hands.

One man came out in chains attached to many different parts of his body. The weight of them allowed him ample opportunity to display his considerable musculature. It was obvious, as he moved, that these were no ordinary theater props. Every motion he made caused a different set of muscle mass to ripple.

But it was the guy in the three-piece suit who took top honors. Using his suit in this segment, he did a totally unexpected striptease down to a skimpy posing strap that turned out to have a necktie painted on it. In the counting he had won no one single event I noticed, but the accumulation of his high rankings just beneath first place in each gave him the trophy at the finale.

After the competition there was a party in one of the local bars. I went, glad to get a chance to meet the men who'd been on stage. I was especially glad to meet Brad, the winner, who was wearing only shoes and the pants from his famous suit. After we shook hands he immediately began to ask me questions about my work.

I explained about the tour and how it had been going so far. His inquiries seemed to have some kind of urgency behind them; he wasn't simply asking me questions to be polite—the way so many other men had since I'd begun this. He wanted some specific answer, but I wasn't quite sure what it was.

Then, when it seemed as though our conversation was just too frustrating, he blurted out, "God, I miss cock."

I stood there for a minute, a little bit stunned. He was looking off into space with an expression of sheer anguish.

"I used to get it all the time. In back rooms, in baths, in parks—you name it. It was there waiting for me. This"—he shrugged his shoulders to let me know he meant his body development—"was just something I started to get more of it. I learned that a big chest and bigger arms were sure to bring you cock. I loved it."

"You still do." One of the other contestants had overheard us talking, and he interjected his opinion. "You just don't know how to get it anymore."

"I know I can't *have* it anymore. That's the torture of it all. You saw James carrying around his chains tonight? Well, that's what I carry around inside me all the time. That's what life's like for me now—life without cock."

"But there are so many options—" I started.

He waved away my protest. "I know there are, and I use them. I know all about rubbers; I could probably give you a more complete lecture on the drawbacks and benefits of the different brands than you've ever heard before. I know all about masturbation—I could write an encyclopedia about masturbation. But I can't get cock anymore. Not like I used to.

"Don't you remember the old days? When you could walk into some place that had dozens of men with their cocks hanging out of their pants? Those *things* would be there, in all different shapes and states of desire, just waiting for a little bit of attention to get them standing up and saluting. God, those were the days. If only I could live them over once more . . ."

He dragged himself back from his dreams. "Oh, I know all about what you're doing, and I think it's great. But there's something about the pleasure of an army of cocks I could get hold of that I miss."

Brad moved away, and I turned to Kip and asked him what was going on. "Well, it's not just that he loved cock. That's the word he uses, but it's a little bit more than that. You see, Brad's one of those guys who came out with the idea that the main thing about sex was to come, as much as possible. He measured his sexual success in the world by the number of loads he could drag out of a group of people.

"He's a great guy, and when he has settled down, he's been a good lover to a couple of guys. But he has this fixation with the stuff. He's very aware of health issues, and he knows that he can't have it anymore. But the idea that he's going to go through life without having all those men pump their stuff inside him or down his throat just drives him crazy.

"You must run into this all the time. Lots of men who adored it must feel a sense of loss like Brad does. But in Brad's mind there's also something more. When you create a symbol, then you have something very, very important in your life. In his own mind he created the symbol that cum was the essence of other men. He wasn't exchanging something as simple as 'body fluids.' He truly perceived cum as *essential* fluids. When the health crisis hit, he was devastated for all the same reasons that the rest of us were. But something special was lost for him as well. So now he channels all of his frustrations and anxieties into the weight lifting."

I thought about what Kip said. I really was back into being Mr. Safe Sex, I realized. If this guy was in trouble, then I was going to have to fly in with my cape—well, my jockstrap—

and provide relief. When I thought about all of the things both Brad and Kip said, I decided I had a remedy that would work more than a little bit.

Drawing on some of my other experiences, I remembered the group-sex session with Terry and Luis and the tremendous sensations I'd gotten as the center of attraction. Then I remembered some of the lessons that Larry had given me about theater. Everything began to gel in my mind. I went around the room, talking with all the guys who'd been in the contest. Just as I'd hoped, I didn't have any trouble convincing them to go along with the idea I'd come up with. I had a suspicion that they were hoping for something sexual to come out of the contest, anyway. My plan was even hotter than they had expected.

After I'd made sure about a few details, I gave Kip and the others a signal. They began to move toward Brad, who was sitting in a corner, his elbows on his knees, a morose look on his face. It wasn't until he was surrounded by a forest of thick, perfectly developed legs that he realized something was up.

"What's going on?" he asked. But Kip wasn't going to give him a chance to do much talking.

Brad may have been the winner, but he was no match for the ensemble of professionals that picked him up. Half a dozen of the contestants lifted Brad up over their shoulders and took him up to the bar's small stage. The front door was locked, fortunately, so only the "in" group involved in the contest remained inside to perform this latest scenario.

The bartender turned off the jukebox. Soon the bar was filled with the sound of a Wagner march, bringing forth images of huge parading teutonic armies. As Brad was put on the floor of the stage, Kip and another man ripped his clothes off, leaving his amazing body naked. James moved toward him with an armful of his chains, and the others helped him attach the heavy links to Brad's wrists and ankles. He was spread-eagled and nude, helpless in front of all the men.

"You won, Brad," I said to him, unzipping my fly. "It seems only fair that you should collect your reward."

He watched me while my cock came out of my pants and I started to stroke it up to a hard erection. He was looking right at my T-shirt, and I knew that he was reminding himself of who I was and what I stood for. "You don't have to worry," I assured him. "This is all by the book. No risk, just cock. You don't have to do without cock," I told him. "On you is fine. And that's just where you're going to get it—all of it."

"Just cock?" He didn't seem to understand what I meant. But as he looked around the circle of behemoths gathered around him, all of them pulling their pants open and displaying a line of erections already happening or else in the making, understanding began to dawn on him.

He ran his tongue over his lips. "Cock," he said, as if he were uttering a sacred mantra, a religious ritual rather than a simple word.

All around him men were beating off. I felt someone reach over and begin to tug at one of my nipples. Turning, I faced the leatherman from the show. He still had his harness on and had taken off his shirt to display it to its full advantage. I looked down at the hand, my gesture meant to let him know that I liked the sensation. Getting the message, he increased the pressure on my flesh.

All around the circle, cocks were showing themselves in full erections. The range of them was amazing—large, small, circumcised, uncut. There were black cocks, Hispanic cocks, pale ones with crowns of blond pubic hair, and ones so dark that they looked like overly thick licorice.

At least twenty-five men stood around the chained victor of the contest. They had curled cocks, straight cocks, arched cocks, dripping cocks, cocks that needed constant spit applied for lubrication. But the main thing was that they were all there—all of the cocks were there for Brad.

He was beginning to get more and more involved in the show. He would look around the circle wildly, watching each one as it progressed toward its inevitable ejaculation. Which one would shoot first? I could tell that he wondered that as he looked around. Which one would drop the biggest deposit on his naked and eager chest?

On him, not in him. That was the game. "He's earned this," I told the group. "The winner gets all the cum in the group. Give it to him. Let him have the spoils of his victory."

There was a loud, guttural sound from the other side of the stage, and the first of the white viscous fluid spurted out onto Brad's chest. It was sent on its way by a thick black cock that seemed to have no end of liquid to give him.

The sight of the ejaculation was the signal for every man to speed up his action. I felt myself getting ready as the leatherman's hand kept up its constant manipulation of my nipples. I looked at him again, ready to stare him down. Before I knew it, his physical actions turned into a contest of wills between us.

That would be something, I thought. I could be in a room with this guy and we could face each other, our erections ready for action. . . .

There was another sound, another cry announcing that Brad was going to get his due. This load was so big and came out of the man with such force that we could all actually hear it splash onto Brad's chest.

I wasn't far behind, but the leatherman beat me to it. Just as I felt myself beginning to pump from way down inside, his hand left my body and I listened to his groans of release. I joined him seconds later, watching as our two streams met to produce a cascade that flowed onto Brad's pubic hair.

All the men were really getting into it now. The few of us who'd led the way moved back and let the rest of them have a better position. Groans and yells of orgasm came with increasing frequency. So did the sounds of men's liquids splattering onto flesh.

"Cock, cock, cock," Brad chanted, his little litany beginning to pick up. It began with the hush of a religious ritual, but it soon became more and more a triumphant hymn.

Finally the last man was able to come while three others had crowded around him and rubbed different sensitive parts of his body to help him along. As I saw the mammoth bodybuilders paying such careful attention to the last holdout, I had a sudden rush of jealousy and anger at myself. If I had held off, I could have been the one who was receiving all that muscular attention!

Finally everyone—including Brad—was finished. Kip unchained Brad from the stage, and we all got something to drink. Our winner sat up, rubbing his hands over the accumulation of fluids on his body. He was mesmerized by the substance on him; he'd had his ritual, and I was glad to see him receive his reward.

"Do you think up this kind of thing all the time?" James asked me while we sipped some mineral water in the corner. The party had regrouped, and the bartender reopened his doors to let in some unsuspecting people who were in the area.

"Well," I said, smiling, "I've been trying to discover the most original ways for us to keep on thriving with our sexuality. Sometimes you have to improvise." I was sure that my drama teacher would have agreed with that. "You just have to go with what emotions exist. It's a question of the raw material.

"I do have to admit, though, that I had no problem with the idea of getting all of you to whip out your cocks and show them off. I could sense that there was a lot of interest in the group here."

"Definitely," James said. "There *was* plenty of interest. I'm not sure that you should go around promoting public sex as a rule, mind you. But I'm glad to see that you still have enough of a sense of the erotic to let things happen so spontaneously. Sometimes I worry that safe sex is all too structured. It can't be just one kind of sex, you know? I mean, that's why we came out, isn't it? To be able to explore sex?"

"You got it, James. That's one of the things that we can't lose in the middle of this crisis: We can't forget that we have always looked at sex in so very many ways. You know, I'm not sure I really would have responded to Brad or anyone else so strongly if I hadn't heard what was said about his having a set of symbols about sex. It made me pay even more attention to him than I might otherwise have done.

"Taking sex out of the closet was why we came out into the open. We can't let this health crisis defeat that goal."

"Well, Mr. Safe Sex," James said, "I think you're pretty well-equipped to show the way."

His hand went to my crotch. "Hey, what was it you were saying about public displays?" I said.

"Well, we don't have to be public. We could go back to my place."

"Those chains of yours aren't my thing."

"We can use them in ways you've never dreamed of—and none of them will be the usual. No heavy stuff, don't worry. *Creative*—that's the key word, isn't it? Let's go get creative in my apartment."

"You're not taking me anyplace I don't want to go?"

"Promise."

CHAPTER THIRTEEN

LONG-DISTANCE INTERCESSION

"Sergeant Swann, sir."

"Hello?" The phone had jolted me out of a deep sleep. The unexpected salutation confused me.

"It's your cadet reporting, sir."

As I struggled to get conscious I recognized Sam's voice over the long-distance wire. "What's going on?" I asked. Stretching under the crisp hotel sheets, I let out a silent yawn.

"I . . . I need to talk to you, sir."

"Yeah?"

"I'm having trouble with discipline, Sergeant Swann."

I was more awake now and could pick up a tremor in Sam's voice. "Tell me about it." I decided to play into his act and added, "Cadet."

"Sir, you know I've been trying to keep up the image you left here in Florida. I've been performing at the local clubs, just the way you told me to. I give lectures for the AIDS group in town. I even did a radio talk show and told the audience all about safe sex."

"I'm proud of you." There was a knock on the door. It had to be the wake-up tray of coffee that I'd ordered before I went to bed the night before. I managed to stand up and pull on my robe without letting Sam know that I wasn't paying full attention to his conversation. Caffeine was more a necessity than a luxury right now.

I made it to the door and gestured the waiter to come inside. He smiled at how unkempt I was, ill-prepared for visitors. I knew he must have been used to it, though. He went about placing the tray on the table and then silently handed me the check and a pen to sign it.

"Well . . ." Sam was having a hard time getting it out.

"Sam, let me know what your problem is."

"I just want to go out and *do* it!" He blurted out his confession with sudden vehemence.

"That's natural. We all want a good hard cock to play with." I was remembering last night's group session for Brad. "You're not the only one who resents the limitations we have. But what you have to do, Sam, is make sure you find enough safe ways to have sex that keep you satisfied. If you don't go out and have fun, you're just going to make yourself frustrated. You're going to let everything build up to a level where you'll start acting without thinking, and you can't do that." Sam's difficulty had absorbed my attention so fully that I only then realized that the waiter hadn't left the room. He was still standing in front of me, listening intently to my passionate speech.

Sam was talking so quickly, and he seemed to be in such a state, that I didn't want to interrupt him just to tell the waiter to leave.

"But what do you *do*?" he said. "I mean, what am I supposed to do? It's early in the morning. I could barely sleep last night, I was so horny. The only thing I could do now is go to a park or something and meet some guy who's going to refuse to take precautions. . . . Sarge, I want sex so badly, I don't know what to do. It just doesn't work to jerk off by myself all the time."

"Sounds like you're just lonely, as much as anything else, Sam."

"Yeah, I'm lonely for the touch of another human being. I wish you were here."

By now the waiter was giving me a very understanding look; the expression in his eyes seemed to echo Sam's wistfulness. Jesus, what a situation!

"Well, I am here," I said. "We can at least communicate with each other. Come on, talk to me."

"I just wish I were with you, Sarge. I mean, if you were around, we could at least have a little training session, you know? And we could at least touch each other." I listened to the sound of Sam's breathing, unmistakably picking up speed.

I have to admit that the sudden change in his voice was having its effect on me too. The remembrance of the "training sessions" we'd gone through went right from my brain to my cock, via the express route. My cock was stirring under the light covering of my robe—and the waiter wasn't missing that little detail.

Sam kept on talking. While I listened to his voice I also was studying the possibilities the waiter was presenting. Well, actually, they weren't possibilities; they were realities—if I wanted them. The way he was studying the growing joint under my robe and the way his own pants were filling out at the crotch was more than enough evidence of that.

"I just wish I could feel a big man's arms around me," Sam was saying. "Besides that, I need a refresher course, Sarge. I mean, I need to be reminded of all the things that we could do that would still be okay—all the things to do if you were here.

"Have you been doing any research? Huh? It would make

things a lot easier if you could tell me the results. Maybe there's something I could use."

I knew perfectly well that Sam expected to "use" whatever I might tell him right then. There was a pattern to his breathing over the phone. I could imagine his blond swimmer's body sprawled out on the bed, one hand holding the telephone while the other worked on a hard cock.

I also knew that the waiter wasn't about to leave. He was standing in front of me, any hint of subtlety gone. His hand had moved to cover the mound of his slacks. Actually, when I thought about it, he looked a bit like Sam. He was light-haired if not actually blond; the shade was more like a dark ash. He was smooth-shaven and about the same age as Sam: in his early twenties.

"So you want to hear about what I did last night?"

I was talking to both of them. Both answered, Sam with a growled "Yeah" and the waiter with an enthusiastic nod of his head.

"I judged this bodybuilding contest."

"You got to see all those men in their posing briefs?" Sam asked the question, but I could tell that the waiter was thinking it.

"Better than that. It was a real contest. The guys got down to little straps that were hardly big enough to hold them. Afterward the winner collected a very special prize. The whole crew stood around him and jerked off on top of him. He wanted cock, and they gave it to him."

"You mean he had all those men's dicks hanging out where he could see and touch them?"

"He couldn't *touch* them, Sam. But he could see them, especially when they shot all over his body."

"They did that? Man, I could just imagine what it would be like to have a shower of cum falling on my stomach, on my balls. . . ."

"Well, he had it."

"Yours too? Huh, Sarge? Did you get into it?"

"Sure I did—I led the way. I had my thing out and jerked it hard and fast."

The waiter seemed to decide that I was giving him instructions as much as retelling a story. He reached inside him and dragged out his own cock. How did a small young man like that ever grow one that big? I wondered.

"Just jerking off, though," Sam was descending back into melancholy.

"Hey, you should never call it just jerking off. Remember, Sam, we're the ones who are teaching people how to do it better. I got some extra lessons in private after that group scene."

"You did? From who? The guy who won?"

"Nah, he was in such a state that he could barely talk afterward. No, Sam, I went home with this leather guy. . . ."

"You went home with someone into S&M? What happened? What did you do to him?" His excited voice changed to a more inquisitive tone. "What did he do to you?"

"Don't get too excited, Sam, I didn't get into an S&M scene. It's not my style." The waiter's face dropped, and I thought I could actually see his cock start to go flaccid after I'd said it, ruining whatever fantasy he'd been working on. "Well, it wasn't a *real* S&M scene. At least not in the usual sense."

"What does that mean?" The excitement was still in Sam's voice, and the waiter picked up his sexual tempo again.

"After the party we went back to his place. He lived in an old victorian house in the Castro district. He had his basement fixed up, the walls covered with leather and all this equipment around. I told him I wasn't into that stuff, but he'd insisted we could have a scene without getting involved in the heavy stuff.

"We stripped down to our skin. He had on a harness, which he did keep on. It had these wide leather straps that crossed over his chest and around his back. They met in one single strap that went down across his belly to his cock in the front and his ass in the back."

By now the waiter had dropped his trousers and removed his shirt. He was nearly hairless and extremely sleek. Holding his balls, he used his other hand to rub his chest and belly where all the flesh was tight and smooth. I had a stereophonic trip going on: Sam's voice and the waiter's physique. They were both getting me going. My cock was hard under the robe, and the waiter knew it all too well.

He knelt down and opened the two parts of the garment to reveal my erection. He went to suck it in his mouth, but I pushed him back, refusing to let him do it right away.

"Yeah." I continued talking to Sam. "This guy had lots of equipment. He says it's the best thing for safe sex he's found. He's a guy who really can't go without getting fucked; that was too much for him to give up. A condom-covered dick could do it for him. But he wanted it so often that he decided he'd invest in some toys. You know, that's one good option we don't tell people about enough.

"You know, Sam, I finally went out and bought a couple of dildos after I talked to this guy. They're still in their wrappers in my suitcase, right on the dresser here in the room."

Getting the message, the waiter jumped up and went to my luggage, rummaging through it until he came back with three models of erect cocks. I kept on talking to Sam but also giving the necessary information to the waiter: "You have to make sure they're clean. That's important. You really should have toys that are only used on yourself. If you have any doubts, well, just insist on a new one all for you."

The waiter looked at his burden and realized that one was still wrapped in the cellophane that it had come in. He put the other ones back in the bag. Then he went about opening up the one he had obvious intentions for. He was naked now and seemed to be totally oblivious to the huge erection that was leading him around the room like a spike.

"This guy was really into them?" Sam clearly didn't want me to linger too long on the precautions right now.

"He sure was. I told you that he had that harness on? Well, those straps that went down the front and back each had an anchor. The one in the front ended in a cock ring that he wore around his cock and balls. It was a heavy metal thing that seemed to keep him half hard all the time.

"At least, I *thought* it was the ring that was doing that. But then he showed me how the rear strap was attached. It ended in a small butt plug that was stuck up his ass. He walked around the whole day with that thing up there, a constant reminder of his sexuality."

"Up his ass all day . . . ?" Sam's voice was trailing off.

"It had a very narrow neck, so it wasn't really doing that much to the sphincter muscles. But inside was a rounded head that kept it stuck in him. He said he didn't wear them all the time, but whenever he wore the harness, to a bar or something, it was there.

"But like I say, it was small. He was really into his toys, and he wanted to show them off to me. He undid the rear strap and removed the butt plug; then he took a nice, long, hard rubber dildo and showed it to me. He got a can of lubricant and greased it up."

So did the waiter.

"He seemed to make love to that thing, as though it were part of *me*. He ran his hands up and down its length for a long time, but he'd stare at me. Even though he knew he couldn't have my own naked cock up his ass, that didn't mean that he and I couldn't have a good time.

"He was putting on a show for me. It was another, more

intense variation on the kind of display you and I have done so often."

And which the waiter was doing right now. As soon as I'd described the way James had worked the dildo, this guy started doing the same thing to me.

"He shoved it up himself right in front of you?" Sam asked.

"He didn't just fuck himself with it, Sam. He turned it into a production. That's the secret of all this, isn't it? That we learn how to make these things all the more exciting? There are lots of things that we might have done in the past that we simply have to make even hotter now.

"This guy was really into it. You have to remember: He's this *big* man. He's into his body so much that he shaves his torso. That's actually one of his S&M fetishes, he told me. He has this trainer at the gym he goes to who turns it into a ritual.

"That's one of the good things about S&M guys: They understand that you can make even simple things hot and horny if you take good care of them and use a little bit of theater as well. This guy's trainer takes him into the shower room every week, and while he gives him a critique of how his development's been going, he uses a razor blade the way another guy might use a pointer. He shaves the man's chest and describes the progress that's been made on the pecs, or he tells him he's been too lazy with his legs while he shaves the calves.

"The thing is, this guy had nothing to hide his body from me—not even hair."

"Not on his cock and balls?"

"Not on his cock and balls and not in the cleft of his ass, either. It was all taken off every week by the trainer.

"So here's this big bodybuilder with muscles that you usually see only in magazines. He's standing there with a huge dildo that's being greased up while his hairless cock is standing there waiting. He tells me he's going to fuck himself for me.

"He did it this way: He took the greased cock and put it on the floor. It had a base broad enough to hold it straight up in the air. He looked me right in the face while he squatted down over it."

"What were you doing? Tell me what you were doing," Sam said. I told him exactly what I had done, and also what I was doing at that very moment.

"I had my cock hard, and I was jerking if off nice and slow so the guy could see it. He was so turned on by it that there was saliva running down his chin." That wasn't true. James hadn't been like that; I added the detail because the waiter was.

"Then, watching me closely, he moved lower and lower," just the way the man in front of me did. "He kept jerking on his dick, too, keeping time with me. When the head of the dildo hit his hole, he closed his eyes with this expression on his face that you wouldn't have believed possible.

"It was amazing to watch these big muscles moving around underneath the restraints of the harness while he went at it. He was moving up and down on the whole length of the rubber thing, fucking himself for me, just the way he said.

"I kept on masturbating, thinking about that stuff up him."

"You just watched?" Sam seemed disappointed. I decided that the visual stuff I'd gone through with James wasn't the trick I should be using on him now. I decided to do some improvisation. But just to make sure it was authentic, I reached over and grabbed the waiter's shoulder and dragged him toward me. I secured the phone in the cleft of my neck. Then I used him to perform the actions I described to Sam.

"No, I did more than watch. I put a hand on the back of his neck and threw him over one of my bare knees so his ass was sticking straight up in the air. Then—come on, this guy was into it, I didn't have to be nice about these things—I spread his legs as far apart as they'd go.

"He still had the dildo up his hole. I took the bottom of it and pulled it nearly out, so just the tip was spearing his sphincter. He moaned out loud when I did that." So did Sam. So did the waiter.

"But I wasn't going to take it out. Instead I shoved it back inside him. I knew he really wanted it, he'd told me so. I didn't pay attention to any of the sounds he made. Once he said, 'Do you have to be so rough?' I asked him, 'Do you want me to be gentle?' When he said, 'No,' I shoved the dildo even harder.

"I could watch the cheeks of his ass as they quivered while I went to town. I was fucking him with that thing as much as I would have been with my own cock. I let it slide in and out of him. After the first couple of times he gave up his game of not liking it.

"He'd lift his ass up higher, as though he were begging me to go even deeper." Well, that's what the waiter did, anyhow. "He moved on my knee, letting me feel his hard cock against my thigh. It was wet from all the precum it had been dripping. He was pressing against me hard.

"I could hold the dildo in one place then. His own movements were enough to keep up the fucking. He was rolling his hips against me. Every thrust he'd make as he rubbed would also make a thrust with the rubber cock. If he moved forward, the cock would slip back out; but when he backed up, he'd impale himself all over again with the thing.

"It went on and on like that until I knew he couldn't hold it in any longer. Then he picked up speed . . ."

The two men I was having sex with both did the same thing. There was no doubt that Sam's heavy breathing was taking him close to the brink. The waiter was moving so fast now that I knew he'd have to explode.

In a matter of seconds I had a double feature: the eruption of Sam's voice in my ear and the waiter's ejaculation on my thigh.

"Oh, Sarge, that was wonderful. I needed that. But you have to get off too. Come on, Sarge, tell me what you're doing to yourself right now."

I didn't think it was necessary to tell him who was doing what, but I certainly had some activity that I could describe. The waiter had slipped off the dildo and had moved to his knees in front of me. He was studying my hard cock reverently.

"I have a hand on my cock and another one holding my balls," I started to say. "I'm pumping my dick nice and slow. I have to do it that way—slow—because I'm so hot, I may come any minute. I love the way my balls feel when I heft them up this way. I like to press them against my body, and I like to pull them down so they can rub against my asshole.

"When I'm doing this, Sam, I put the heels of my feet up on the arms of my chair. I get my ass wide open so I can run my sac right over the beginning of the crack. Then I can run my hand all the way up and down the cleft if I want to. Yeah . . . I want to.

"I'm getting really close now. I can feel it starting to move inside me . . ."

"Ah, come on, Sarge, shoot a load for me. I can just picture it. I can see my face right up to the side of your erection. I can watch it getting ready. Are you really close?"

"I'm really, really close. I know it's going to happen, Sam. I know it's coming . . . *now!*"

The waiter brought a towel that he'd wet with warm water from the bathroom and wiped me clean. Then he began to put his clothes back on. I was still talking to Sam.

"You should call whenever you want to, guy. This phone sex is one of the best ways to get into things safely, especially at strange times of the day. You know, there are a couple of networks that people have started up just for this. You can call anytime, and they'll connect you with men who are ready and willing to talk dirty enough to get you off."

"But, Sarge, aren't those things too expensive?"

"They're not all commercial. Some are really different. They're really just networks. Sometimes you might want to talk to a pro; other times you can just find a phone buddy in the personals or something, and you'll be able to call each other when you need to. Whatever. The talking's just another way to get it off."

The waiter was getting it all off now. He smiled, reached down, and patted my exhausted cock as his own way of saying good-bye. I didn't even know his name!

"What about the toys, Sarge? When you get back to Florida, will you teach me about toys?"

"I don't need to be there to do that, Sam. We can talk about them. There are stores around where you can go and buy all kinds of things."

"Well, you know, I guess I really meant that I hoped you'd do even more. I was thinking, maybe we could have a dildo that was just mine. If I could look forward to having you break it in with me, just the way you described, then I'd have something to anticipate, you know? I could think about getting fucked by you with that thing. . . ."

"Sure, Sam!" I had a lot of enthusiasm in my voice. It might have had a lot to do with watching the waiter wave a final good-bye and closing the door behind him as he left.

"And then, when you're on the road again and I got to be this horny, I could call you up and you could talk to me while I fuck myself again with *your* dildo. . . ."

"You're on, man," I said. "We'll go shopping together,

and we can find an extra-special one. Just the two of us this time."

" 'This time'?" He asked. "What do you mean?"

"Um . . . nothing, kid. Nothing. I was just getting all excited about our little shopping trip and the phone conversations we're going to be having. It'll help me, too, Sam. There are some times when I could use a familiar voice myself. So, we're in this together, right?"

"Yes, sir, Sarge!"

CHAPTER FOURTEEN

FINAL TOUCHES

"Well, that's quite a story. I'm not sure what to make of it. On one level it's a reaffirmation that those spontaneous moments of anonymous sex we used to revel in don't have to be lost. And you certainly are right about there being advantages to phone sex. But you seemed to have combined your elements a little bit too much."

"Arthur, you're just being shortsighted. You just want the world to conform to how we do it. I think Glenn's little adventure this morning had just the right touch—so to speak."

We were sitting in a great restaurant at the top of Nob Hill. George and Arthur, his lover, were taking me to dinner after I'd given still another performance. I had just finished a huge meal and was sitting back enjoying the sensation of being totally satisfied.

"Actually, George, maybe we should tell Glenn just how we do handle it," Arthur went on.

The two lovers smirked at each other, obviously enjoying their little conspiracy. I waited to see what would happen. Evidently George had decided to take seriously my lecture about being open and honest on matters of sex. He began to explain.

"Arthur and I came out together in college. We've been together for fifteen years." That surprised me. They looked so young, I had assumed that they could have been lovers for only a short time.

"When we graduated, we moved here from Texas in order to get into the gay life we'd heard so much about. In San Francisco we were able to learn and share a lot of things. We really have become members of a *community,* and that's something we've appreciated.

"That's not to say we overlooked the sexual opportunities the city has to offer. After talking about it we agreed that monogamy was not the way to best appreciate ourselves and this city."

"At least not at the beginning," Arthur said. For a minute we all sat quietly. Anyone who was out and sexually active in San Francisco during the past few years must feel just plain lucky to be alive now, I thought, more so than in the rest of the country. We all were thinking the same thing, I knew; not a word had to be spoken.

"Well . . ." George picked up the conversation again. "We went through all the things that most lovers do. We finally agreed to our own patterns of how to keep our relationship going and our sexual needs met. When events made us include some . . . alterations, we did what we had to in order to keep our health. But we always had a broad definition of health. We knew that it had to include our entire physical existence."

"Including sex," Arthur said emphatically.

"Especially including sex," George agreed. "We had to make sure that the virus wasn't killing off our sexual health as well. That's the bottom line—that is, it became the bottom line.

"A couple of years ago I got a big promotion at work," he went on. "It was something I'd been striving for since I'd graduated, and both of us knew that I would have to take it, even though it meant that I'd have to travel much more than we were used to."

"Another time, another decade," Arthur said, joking, "I'd have jumped at the chance to have all that spare time here in San Francisco. I just imagined what it would have been like: one week I have a committed lover at home with me doing all the domestic things that we both enjoy; the next week I could be down on Folsom Street having a ball with all those men. But . . ."

" 'But' is right," George said. "There are the options you talk about, Glenn. And I'm glad you do. But even with the things we can still do, I think there's less glamour in it all. So I suddenly discovered that what I had was a great promotion and a very unhappy lover. He didn't want to go out and trick the way he would have several years ago. He began to resent our separations—and that put a lot of unpleasant pressure on us."

"Until we discovered just what your friends did: the phone and the toys." Arthur looked at his lover expectantly.

"It began by accident," George said. "One week I was in Denver, and Arthur seemed to be more and more anxious and bitchy each time we talked. I started to get angry with him—I even threatened him in one conversation. We didn't usually argue, but all of a sudden I had to warn him about how I was going to take care of him in order that he wouldn't be so out of control the next time I left home. That really got to him.

"It ended up being the greatest jerk-off session we ever had together—and we were hundreds of miles apart when it happened."

Arthur picked up the story: "It was all I needed. I went down to all the sex shops on Folsom Street and in the Tenderloin and discovered a million different options that we hadn't ever explored. One of them is our own special version of what you've described. It was a kit. You can use it to make a cast of someone's cock and then create a personal dildo from it.

"As soon as George came home, believe it or not, I stripped him naked and threw him on the kitchen table. Then I used all the little things I'd discovered over the years to get him hard. After this long you do learn those tricks.

"When he was stiff, I kept him that way with little recreations of times we'd had in the past that I knew he'd especially loved. Even though he complained about the feel of the mold and how difficult it was to maintain his hard-on while I was trying to make it, I managed to keep it erect for long enough to get my impression.

"After that . . . well, when I get the urge and he's out of town on business, I create this whole scenario in preparation for the call I know is going to come at night. I'm all set up with my absolutely authentic replica of my sweetheart's cock. I grease it up and shove it inside and listen to his voice. . . ."

"It's not the real thing, but it still is hot. I know the real thing's always coming home to me eventually, anyway, and that's something that makes it easier for me to handle."

We laughed over their improvisation. "Well, I'm glad you guys worked that out."

"I don't think it's all that difficult. When you think about it, really, we'd be facing a lot of the same issues in a different time, even if the health concerns weren't the same. That's one thing that a lot of people forget. They blame *all* their sexual problems on the virus. That's not the whole truth. What we just described still would be something that any two lovers might have to go through if their work kept them apart," George said.

"I guess the observation I'd make," Arthur added, "is that having a lover creates a different situation. How do you handle your private life, Glenn?"

I wondered if I would have minded the personal question a few years earlier. I didn't now; I understood that it was coming from someone who was concerned and interested. It wasn't just an invasion of privacy. I told them all about the things that had happened to me since I'd been Mr. Safe Sex.

I had a lot of good things going, I told them. I had learned about my body and how to have sex with it in more adventuresome ways than I ever would have attempted before. That, and I had learned to make sex something even more special than it had ever been to me.

I wasn't going to deny that I'd had problems. I explained how I had made a mistake—it was a mistake for *me*, though it didn't have to be for someone else—and had gotten too far out with impersonal sex for a while. I had forgotten some of the benefits that touching and affection could bring me.

But Yato had brought me back. That also had made me remember that the things done spontaneously were also events I enjoyed. I just had to keep the balance between orgasmic exploration and personal need. I had to remember all the ways to take care of myself.

I thought that the next big tour would be easier. I told George and Arthur that I understood the ways I was capable of taking care of myself. I'd make sure I had more time alone, more quiet time for my emotions as well as my body.

I really was looking forward to getting back to Miami, I realized. That was certain. For me Miami was the place where all of the things I needed could be gotten most easily. Even when sexual adventures were involved, they took place with people I knew. I could get off on something like the phone call with Sam I'd described, but I also knew that Sam and I could just cuddle when that was called for too.

"Seems like you need to do more than just have Mr. Safe Sex substitutes in all the cities you tour," George told me. "You should also have a little network of Mr. Safe Sex rest spas just for yourself. You talk about the balance that's necessary in your erotic and emotional life. Well, let's find you some islands where you can get the R and R that allows you to keep up the rest of it."

I didn't quite get what George was saying. My confusion must have been obvious, because Arthur went on to explain.

"George and I want you to consider our home your own, Glenn, when you come to San Francisco next time. George travels more than enough to understand how impersonal hotel rooms can be. And he's offering our bodies as our intimate sacrifice to the movement."

Arthur was laughing. "You're getting a safe-sex come-on, and you don't even know it. We've been wanting to get it on with you since we met you. You've been so open and honest with us as you described your likes and dislikes and your needs that you've walked right into our hands. Our own tastes match your program awfully well."

George reached over and put his hand over mine. "How about coming back to our apartment tonight? Your tour's over. You're going home soon. Why not start your rest and relaxation? Let us take care of Mr. Safe Sex for a change. We'll put you in a good mood—it's time to let you celebrate a little bit."

"That's okay with you guys?" I said. "You make it sound as though you were just into each other these days."

"We like to share, Glenn. It's one of our favorite things. If another guy likes us and understands that our special emotional relationship is our private affair, then we have lots of room in our lives for other special people who can deal with being a part of it."

Both George and Arthur were very honest about their desires. Having sex with someone else was something they used in order to increase their joint pleasure. I appreciated that, and it made sense to me too. I'd been in some three-ways with other couples where there was tension and it was obvious that one or the other—or both of them—were using the situation just to get in another man's pants. But every aspect of this triangle was different.

When we entered the apartment, we all kissed and embraced. We moved right into the bedroom where the lighting had obviously been designed for optimal sensual effect.

I finished undressing first. I was on the bed waiting for them as I watched them get out of their clothes. While they had been appreciative of me and my body—no doubt about that—they were totally involved when they studied each other. I wasn't exactly excluded, but there was no doubt that something special was going on between them that was all their own.

Arthur was a redhead. He had only a little bit of hair on his torso, and its wheatlike color was almost lost against his skin. George was dark-haired. He had a vast mat of hair over his chest that dove into a small funnel as it moved to his belly.

Without being "developed" in the same sense as the guys I'd seen at the contest they were both well-built. Their stomachs were tight and their asses nicely rounded; I could see that the flesh there was firm. They were about as tall as I was, and they were both well-proportioned, bulky in perfect relation to their height.

Once I saw how very much involved they were in their partnership, I wondered how they would be able to include me in it. I soon found out that I needn't have been so concerned.

When they were naked, I watched them embrace. They were both getting hard already, and their thickening cocks were pressed between their bellies. The tips slipped over to the side, as if they were pointing to me. The embrace was the last private moment from which I was excluded.

As soon as they were finished, they moved over to the bed, placing their bodies on mine. Suddenly there was this mass of flesh and hair all around me. Hands I couldn't identify were exploring me with soft and gentle caresses. Hard and slippery cocks were everywhere, sliding around, and soft, hair-covered balls were pressing against my legs. There were mouths all around, many legs intertwining.

I had expected that they were just going to get to it. There certainly was enough sexual energy in the room to propel most people to a fast and furious session, after all. But that wasn't what they had in mind.

Moving their bodies away from me at the same time, they withdrew. I felt hands reaching under my body and rolling me over onto my stomach. Someone opened a drawer somewhere; the sound was accompanied by the sensation of hands caressing me.

Then I felt the first touch of warm lotion being spread over my ass. My buttocks felt compliant. More hands—again covered with lotion—were moving over my shoulders, and I could sense the resistance and strength of my own muscles.

"Isn't this how you began, Glenn? With a massage?"

I moaned a yes.

The hands moved over me so expertly and so firmly that I couldn't even be sure that there were only four of them.

"What was it you progressed to? Rubbing against another man? And then exhibiting yourself? Wasn't there a lesson in rubbers in there as well? Fucking and getting fucked with protection?"

"Ummmm . . ."

"And there was recruiting all those Mr. Safe Sex guys around the country. Hard work, Glenn, making sure that they were equipped well enough to carry off the work that needed to be done. That was very hard work. We wonder how much of that you could fit into one night? We have a lot of time ahead of us. We could just stick with the massage or get into some heavier stuff. Whatever you want, Glenn. This is your night."

"And all those fantasies you had to think up! Try this one on: In addition to the other recruiting you do, add getting a special place for Glenn Swann in every city. A place where he can come and relieve the tensions, get a good massage, just a back rub if he wants it."

"Or more—maybe a heavy session with some toys of his own that he can keep there and know are clean and safe."

"Or else a quiet session where he can just lay back and get a good fucking when he needs it."

"Or know that there's a guy waiting who's going to let him do the fucking."

"Think of all the fantasies you want, Glenn; just make sure they're all for yourself and no one else."

The hands moved more and more firmly up and down my body, over my limbs, delving into the crack of my ass.

"It's such a hard job being Mr. Safe Sex," George said to Arthur. "Just think of all the people he has to make happy." I had a suspicion that the voice belonged to the finger that was moving into my moist and relaxed sphincter. I realized that these guys were going to be willing to do it all if I let them. They were right; it *was* such a hard job being Mr. Safe Sex. But I couldn't think about all that now. I had taken them at their word; I wasn't even trying to remember what was going on. This was for me. I don't have to recreate every fantasy I undertake for the whole world, I told myself. I have the right just to lie back and feel those hot sexual messages up and down my body. . . .

"*Ummm . . .*"

And who said sex in the eighties couldn't be sensational?